DANGEROUS CROSSING

I'd been walking for half an hour. That should have put me at midspan. Judging from the cluster of people there, that was exactly the point I'd reached. Dozens of cameras were pointed in every direction.

I slowly turned to take in 360 degrees of my surroundings. To my left were the hills of Sausalito and Marin County. With my back to the bridge railing, I could see over the traffic to the vast expanse of the Pacific Ocean. And then I returned to my original position, peering out over San Francisco Bay and across to the City by the Bay. It was like an Impressionist painting.

What happened next was hardly impressionistic. It was more out of the school of "Art Brute"—brutal realism.

I felt the strength of a hand, connected to a strong arm, grasp the back of my neck and shove me forward. Simultaneously, another hand—presumably belonging to the same person—grabbed the bottom of my Windbreaker and attempted to pick me up and over the railing. . . .

MARTINIS & MAYHEM

A *Murder, She Wrote* Mystery

A Novel by Jessica Fletcher
and Donald Bain
based on the
Universal television series
created by Peter S. Fisher,
Richard Levinson & William Link

A SIGNET BOOK

For Ted Chichak, who gives all agents a good name

SIGNET
Published by the Penguin Group
Penguin Books USA Inc., 375 Hudson Street,
New York, New York 10014, U.S.A.
Penguin Books Ltd, 27 Wrights Lane, London W8 5TZ, England
Penguin Books Australia Ltd, Ringwood, Victoria, Australia
Penguin Books Canada Ltd, 10 Alcorn Avenue,
Toronto, Ontario, Canada M4V 3B2
Penguin Books (N.Z.) Ltd, 182–190 Wairau Road,
Auckland 10, New Zealand

Penguin Books Ltd, Registered Offices:
Harmondsworth, Middlesex, England

First published by Signet, an imprint of Dutton Signet,
a division of Penguin Books USA Inc.

 REGISTERED TRADEMARK—MARCA REGISTRADA

Printed in the United States of America

PUBLISHER'S NOTE
This is a work of fiction. Names, characters, places, and incidents either are the
product of the author's imagination or are used fictitiously, and any resemblance to
actual persons, living or dead, events, or locales is entirely coincidental.

Chapter One

People who don't know Maine suffer from the delusion that it never gets hot there. They have this vision of perpetually cool summers and bitterly cold winters. But never heat, at least the way it's experienced farther south, and in the big cities.

Their assumption is wrong. Sure, it seldom heats up in Cabot Cove as it does in New York City, or Newark, or Washington, D.C. (no place gets as hot as Washington, D.C., in the summer, except perhaps Bombay, or Death Valley).

But we do have our moments. As evidence, I offer August 17 of last year. It was 70 degrees when I awoke at six. I didn't catch the humidity reading, but my damp skin told me the air had reached its saturation level. One more percentage point of moisture and the dam would burst. It was a Maine heat wave, pure and simple, one of those days when my hair wouldn't need artificial resuscitation to bring its curl back to life.

We'd been in the grips of record-breaking heat for three days, and it had begun to make people edgy. Everywhere I went I heard complaints: "Godfrey mighty! Ain't this heat a killer? Haven't seen anything so jo-jeezly since eighty-seven."

It's all in the mind, I reminded myself as I put on the kettle for tea, and settled in my den to watch *The Today Show*. Willard Scott, my favorite weatherman, was tipping his toupee to a woman in Georgia celebrating her 106th birthday. His enthusiasm was contagious; I started to laugh as he switched to interviewing kids, whose mixed-breed dogs were entered in a show for non-purebreds, my favorite animals. And then it was on to the weather map, and his "pick city" of the day: *San Francisco*. I let out a small cheer because the weather in that jewel of a city was forecast to be a crisp, delightful 71 dry degrees, and was expected to remain that way throughout the weekend and into a good part of the next week.

The reason for my armchair cheer was that I would be there to enjoy it. I was scheduled to leave for San Francisco the following morning to publicize my latest murder mystery, *Blood Relations*. The lure of San Francisco is always strong for me. But considering the difference in weather between there and Cabot Cove, the contemplation of the trip was especially delicious. A vision of enjoying succulent crab claws on Fisherman's Wharf, and watching the cool, mysterious fog envelop the Golden Gate Bridge brought a smile to my face. "Better pack," I said aloud as I peeled myself from the burgundy vinyl recliner in response to the whistling tea kettle.

Usually, I'm packed well in advance of a trip. But the heat and humidity had been a deterrent. The past couple of days had been marked by a distinct lack of productivity in all things. Not much is air-conditioned in Cabot Cove, including my house (I suppose even *we* buy the myth of heat waves only happening in other places, despite knowing better). I'd dug out fans from the attic and set them up in strategic places. They helped; at least they kept the hot, heavy air moving.

I went into the kitchen and poured the steaming water into a large copper pitcher already filled with several herbal tea bags. The room was now a sauna with the additional steam from the kettle. I went outside and placed the pitcher on a table on my brick patio, where the sun would steep it to perfection. After that it would go into my refrigerator. By lunchtime, I'd have an ample supply of homemade iced tea that would impress even Martha Stewart. My iced tea had earned quite a following in town. If I bottled it for sale, the advertisement would read: *Steeped the natural way in the glorious, bountiful Maine sun.* And probably have the FTC after me.

Still in my nightgown, I was in the process of dragging a large suitcase from a hall closet when the doorbell rang. I peeked through lace curtains covering my front bay window and saw the patrol car belonging to Cabot Cove's sheriff, Mort Metzger, parked in my driveway. Even though Mort and I have been friends for years, and he's pulled into my driveway hundreds of times, my heart always

...

skips a beat when I see his official car arrive, afraid that this is the one time he's not paying a social call, but is bringing some sort of bad news.

I threw on a pastel pink robe over my nightgown, and opened the door.

"Gorry, Jess, it's hot," he said, dramatically wiping his forehead with the back of his hand. "Eight-thirty in the morning and already it's eighty-five. Can't hardly breathe with the humidity. Not fit for man or beast."

"Especially beasts," I said. "With all that fur. Come in. The fans are going full tilt."

He continued to complain as he stepped inside. "I'll tell you one thing, Jessica, timing is everything, like they say. You are one lucky lady to be leavin' this tomorrow. Give anything to climb on that plane with you. Watched *The Today Show* this mornin'. Willard Scott, he picked San Francisco as havin' the best weather in the whole darn country. High out there only supposed to get up to about seventy."

"Seventy-one," I said, smiling.

"Well, whatever," he said. "I was on my way to work but couldn't stop thinkin' about a cool, tall glass of Jessica Fletcher's iced tea." He took off his hat and headed straight for the kitchen table.

"You're right, Mort. Timing *is* everything. And you're too early. The iced tea won't be ready until lunchtime."

"I suppose a tall glass of ice water would do," he said grumpily, sitting and plopping his broad-brimmed tan Stetson hat on the table.

"Weather's got you in a foul mood," I said, taking a glass from a cabinet.

"Can't expect much otherwise," he said. "Put plenty of ice in it. Can't get much that's worthwhile done in this weather. My damn uniform is stickin' to me like it was glue. Already got that damn heat rash all over my chest. Run out of the medicine Dr. Hazlitt gave me. I'm itchin' like a thousand no-see-ums got under my shirt."

"Here you go, Mort. A nice glass of cold water with plenty of ice."

"Much obliged."

"Will I see you at lunch? Seth said he'd be over about noon."

"Will the tea be ready by then?" he asked in the same sort of serious tone used when reading someone his rights.

"Yes."

"Then, you can count on me bein' here, Jess. Can't miss your goin'-away lunch, can I?"

"Or my iced tea."

He drained his glass and stood. "Well, got to be running along. Damn car'll overheat if I hit traffic. Got tourists all over the place. Think they'd stay home in this kind of weather. Car's been actin' up lately. Got a radiator problem."

"Not a good thing for a police car," I said, walking him to the door.

"These tourists buzz around in their cars with their air conditioners goin' full-blast. A fella would think they'd melt without their AC. Thanks for the water, Jess. See you later."

I watched him get into his car and curse under his breath as he touched the hot steering wheel. Nothing like a heat wave to bring out the worst in people, I thought.

And nothing like a trip to breezy San Francisco to get away from it.

"This is, hands down, the best iced tea I've ever had, Jess," said Seth Hazlitt, physician and friend of long-standing. He'd approached the mug of amber liquid as if he were tasting fine wine. First he breathed in its aroma, then gently swished it around in the mug before ingesting a small amount with an audible slurp. He allowed the tea to linger, swishing it around in his mouth before swallowing. For a moment, I was afraid he was going to go all the way with his tasting ritual, which would have dictated spitting the tea out rather than swallowing it. The only handy "spittoon" was a bucket of ice I'd placed on the table. He spared me that.

"Lovely lookin' lunch," he said, taking in the platter of cold cuts and assorted salads.

"Leave room for dessert," I said. "Sherbert and fresh fruit salad."

As we ate, talk turned to my trip to San Francisco.

"How long will you be there?" Seth asked, refilling his plate with Virginia ham and shrimp salad, and taking another piece of crusty fresh-baked French bread from Sassi's Bakery.

"About a week. It'll be a busy one. I've got a full schedule of book signings, cocktail receptions, and publicity meetings. I've also committed myself to the Women's Correctional Facility outside San Francisco."

Mort put down his large mug of iced tea and asked, "What on earth are you talking about?"

"Writing," I said. "I'll be speaking to some of the inmates about writing."

Seth winked at me and threw Mort a smile.

"Makes sense, I suppose," he said.

"Apropos," Seth said. "Can't think of a better place to be discussin' how to write murder mysteries."

"That's not what I'll be talking about exactly," I said. "Actually, I'm going to focus on journal writing. You know, writing about feelings, drawing from personal events and experiences."

"How come?" Mort asked.

"Because I truly believe in prison reform. Journal writing could be an important part of that reform. Sometimes you never know you have certain feelings about something until you see them in black and white, on paper."

"I suppose," said Mort, reluctantly. "Only it seems to me, we try to do too much rehabilitatin' and not enough punishin'."

"Two ways to look at it," said Seth.

And a debate was launched over the role of prisons. I used the opportunity to clear the table, and to pack a few more things. When I returned from the bedroom, a truce had been called and the conversation was back to less controversial subjects.

"I was toyin' with the idea of goin' to Frisco myself this weekend," Mort said.

"Really?" I said.

" 'Course, it's too late now. Had to sign up for the seminar a month or two ago."

"And what seminar would that be?" Seth asked.

"On law enforcement. Sponsored by the FBI. All the big shots will be there. Sort of an annual thing. I went to it once, about five years ago. Down in Houston, Texas. Learned an awful lot, and the parties were pretty good. Haven't been back, though. Haven't been able to get away."

"I remember when you went," I said. "Did you say it's sponsored by the FBI?"

"Yup."

"Hmmm," I said. "I wonder if my friend George Sutherland will be attending?"

Mort and Seth exchanged looks. "Friend?" Seth said, pixie in his voice and smugness on his round face.

"Yes, *friend*," I said.

"Why not give him a call," Mort suggested. "Find out."

"I think I will," I said. "*After* you're both on your way."

George Sutherland was, indeed, a friend, although I'd be less than honest not to admit that I sometimes wished our relationship would blossom beyond simple friendship. I'd never expressed this to Mort and Seth, but they knew. My tone of voice, I suppose, when speaking of George; and my tendency to talk too much about him. All those telltale signs that people who know you well pick up on.

We met in London a few years ago. I was addressing a conference of mystery writers, and staying with an old and dear friend and colleague, Marjorie Ainsworth. At that time Marjorie was the reigning queen of the mystery genre. Tragically, she was murdered in her mansion while I was a houseguest, and I ended up being dragged into solving her murder. That's when George Sutherland entered my life.

George is an inspector for Scotland Yard, in London. He's Scottish by birth, his family having come from the northern town of Wick. He's urbane, handsome, charming, and displays a quick wit. Ooops. There I go again waxing poetic about him.

You might think in listening to me—Seth and Mort certainly do—that I've fallen in love with George Sutherland. That isn't true. Nor does he love me. We don't know each other well enough for that to have happened.

But we do have a strong, and mutual respect and liking for each other. And we both know—and I realize I'm speaking for him—that were we to decide to explore whether our relationship might move to another plateau, the chances are good that it would make that leap.

For now, Inspector George Sutherland and mystery writer Jessica Fletcher were content to keep in touch across the vast Atlantic Ocean by letter and by phone. Good friends. Nothing more.

"Mort, do you have information on when and where the law enforcement seminar is being held?" I asked.

"I think I saved the invitation. I get one every year. I'll look for it when I get back to the office and give you a call."

"Hello. This is Jessica Fletcher. I wonder if you could help me. I'm curious if . . ."

"The mystery writer?"

"Yes."

"Oh, boy. My wife won't believe this."

"I'll write a letter if that will help."

"You will? That'd be great."

"I was curious whether an old friend of mine will be attending the conference next week. His name is Sutherland. Inspector George Sutherland of Scotland Yard, London."

"Oh, yes, ma'am, Mrs. Fletcher. Inspector Sutherland usually attends every year. By the way, my name's Ted Wilcox. Special Agent, FBI, San Francisco office. I'm in charge of registration for the conference."

"It's a pleasure to talk to you, Agent Wilcox."

"Would you like to register, Mrs. Fletcher? It's been closed for a few weeks, but for you I'd be happy to make an exception."

"Oh, no, no. I'll be in San Francisco next week and thought I'd look Inspector Sutherland up. We—

we were involved together in a case in London a few years ago."

"Sounds interesting. Want me to leave a message for him on our message board?"

"Not necessary. I'll catch up with him when I can. My schedule is going to be insane. Thanks again."

"No problem, Mrs. Fletcher. I love your books."

I thanked him, hung up, and smiled. What a pleasant surprise it would be to see George again. I did wonder why he hadn't called to tell me he'd be in the United States. I'm sure he had his reasons. No matter. The trip to San Francisco was looking better all the time.

Chapter Two

"*Welcome aboard, ladies and gentlemen. This is your captain from the flight deck. We expect our trip to San Francisco today to take a little less time than scheduled because of the absence of any significant head winds. We will experience a slight delay here at the gate, but it shouldn't be too long. Sit back and relax. We hope you'll enjoy your trip with us, and if there's anything we can do to make it more pleasant, just let us know.*"

"Can I get you a drink, Mrs. Fletcher?"

I don't consider myself an extravagant person, but I do love to fly first-class. Not only is the service better—here we were still on the ground and I was already being asked if I wanted a drink—but I always experience less jet lag after flying up-front. Maybe it's psychological, but the more pleasant the trip is, the less problem I have adjusting to the time difference and its effect upon my circadian body rhythms.

"That would be lovely. A Perrier with lime."

The drink was welcome because the cabin was

stuffy. I browsed the in-flight magazine, wanting to order everything advertised in it, skimmed that morning's *Boston Globe* provided by the flight attendant, considered dragging my new toy, a Compac Contura laptop computer, from beneath the seat in front of me but decided work could wait, and chose instead to begin reading a book I'd brought along. I clumsily dug it out from my oversize Chanel-spin-off black bag, and read the complimentary comments about the book on the front and back covers provided by other authors. The book was called *Scarlet Sins,* and was written by an old friend, Neil Schwartz. Everyone seems to be old friends of mine these days, both in age and duration of friendship.

Neil and I shared a special relationship, having both lost spouses in the same month. I'd drawn a lot of strength from his friendship during that time. Without him, my mourning and healing processes might have been even more painful, and gone on a lot longer.

We'd spent many afternoons and evenings together. So many, in fact, that people began to talk. We shared memorable dinners on those first long, frigid Maine winter nights when I would still automatically set the table for two.

But soon, as often happens, time took its course, and our co-dependent relationship—no negative connotation—began to fade, aided by Neil's announcement one evening at dinner that he was moving back to his roots in Wisconsin where his daughter and grandchildren lived. We kept in touch, but it wasn't the same.

Then, last week, this copy of his book arrived, inscribed to me by Neil: *"To my dear friend Jessica Fletcher, whose only crime is in living so many hundreds of miles away."*

Scarlet Sins was a collection of true murder cases. I opened to the first chapter, which was about a British-born woman, Kimberly Steffer, accused of the murder of her husband, Mark Steffer. I certainly recognized her name, and remembered reading bits here and there about the murder, and the subsequent trial at which she was convicted. She'd made a name for herself as the author of children's books. But not children's books as we generally think of them. Kimberly Steffer wrote stories centering around children's causes and issues—poverty, abuse, single-parent households—themes reflecting the reality of the contemporary child's world.

How sad, I thought, for her to have ended up a convicted murderess. Incredible how very talented people can destroy their lives in the name of love.

For some reason, I didn't want to read, at least not at that moment, about a famous writer murdering her husband. I'd have to be in a different mood for that. I skipped to the next murder case covered in Neil's book and began reading.

The case in Chapter Two was familiar to me, thanks to network television movies based upon the incident. It was the story of two brothers serving life sentences for having killed their sister. The three siblings were actually triplets. The boys' defense lawyers claimed during their separate trials that their triplet sister was the one who'd been spared years of physical and sexual abuse heaped upon the brothers by their parents. They said she'd repeatedly threatened them that if they went to the authorities to tell of the abuse, she'd deny that it ever happened. Without her corroboration, no one would believe them.

I closed the book, closed my eyes, and was sadly pondering all the dreadful things that can happen in people's lives, when we were pushed away from the gate and headed for an active runway. I was glad no one sat next to me because as I looked out the small window at the steam rising from the ground, at the barren strips of runway, with half-dead weeds and dandelions, I thought of my dead husband and started to cry softly. It had been a long time since I cried for him. I didn't fight it. I knew that it was all part of the process, and probably long overdue.

My tears stopped as the captain applied maximum thrust and we rolled down the runway. Moments later we were airborne and climbing to our announced cruising altitude. I freshened up in a lavatory, returned to my seat, opened my laptop, and went to work. I needed to think about things less gruesome than brothers killing sisters and wives killing husbands, something light like the outline for my next murder mystery. At least it's fiction. The blood isn't real, although I always try to make it sound as though it is.

I napped after lunch. As I dozed off, I thought of Neil Schwartz, of his book, and of the support we'd found in each other after the death of our respective spouses.

True crime was not Neil's genre. Most of his writing had resulted in books of poetry, published by small, off-the-beaten-path publishers. But Neil had been a New York City cop before retiring to Maine to indulge his love of poetry. His experiences on the mean streets of Manhattan gave his poetry an edge that set it apart. Of course, it was a good thing he had his cop's pension. Poetry writing doesn't pay many bills.

While others watched the movie, I went back to my laptop and the outline for my next book. Before I knew it, the captain informed us we were beginning our descent into foggy San Francisco.

"Is San Francisco your final destination?" asked Eric, one of the flight attendants working the flight. I knew his name from the silver-winged name tag he wore. He leaned on the armrest of the unoccupied seat next to me.

"Yes. And happily so. It's one of my favorite cities."

"Mine, too," he said. "Well, better bring your seat back up, Ms. Fletcher. We'll be landing in a minute."

The captain came back on the public address: *"Folks, I've got good news for you. It's a beautiful seventy-one degrees in San Francisco. Couldn't ask for a better forecast. It's been a pleasure serving you. If you're continuing on with us, we'll look forward to carrying you to your next destination. If not, enjoy your stay in the City by the Bay."*

My confidence in Willard Scott's weather forecasts affirmed, I gathered my things. Music was piped into the cabin—Tony Bennett's *I Left My Heart in San Francisco*. And I couldn't help but think of Scotland Yard Inspector George Sutherland.

I found the limo driver who'd been dispatched by my publisher to drive me into town, breathed in the cool, invigorating air as he held open the door for me, and sat back in the spacious rear seat and sighed.

Sometimes, things are so good you can hardly stand it.

Chapter Three

One Week Later

The Queen of England had once stayed in my suite at the Westin St. Francis. Although I pride myself in not overly responding to celebrity, I must admit to a certain thrill at walking the same floors as that regal lady, tracing the footsteps of a Who's Who of world leaders and dignitaries.

It was called the Windsor Suite, on the thirty-first floor. I didn't dare ask what my publisher was paying for it, although I did eventually learn that it went for $1500 a night, a queenly sum. Its views were splendid: I looked out over Union Square to the downtown area, and to Coit Tower on Telegraph Hill. I could see the Bay Bridge to Oakland, and the lovely bay it spanned. The Santa Cruz Mountains near San Jose were also visible.

There was a large dining room, a sumptuous bedroom, living room, baths the size of my living room back home, and a second bedroom off the dining room that also opened into a second suite on the floor, the Bayview Suite, slightly smaller but no less opulent.

My goodness, I thought, slightly embarrassed by having been given such a wonderful suite, and for all the fuss made of my visit by the hotel staff. I gave myself a tour, stopping to inhale the lovely aroma of two dozen red roses that graced a coffee table, and to sample from a platter overflowing with fruit and cheese and other delectables that sat temptingly on the bar.

The hotel itself, I knew, was considered one of the world's finest. That assessment by world travelers received no argument from this lady.

The week had flown by, as busy weeks always tend to do. My schedule was choreographed by a well-informed and highly organized publicist, Camille Inken, with whom I had dinner almost every night. Camille was a petite thirty-five-year-old with ink-black hair and a delicate, dusty rose complexion. Her calf muscles were like a ballerina's; so many women in San Francisco build shapely legs trudging up and down its fabled hills.

When I felt comfortable enough with Camille, I asked if she was married and had a family. She said without any defensive regret or sadness, "No time for that in this job, Jessica. Maybe someday, but not right now." She had, to my ear, the hint of a Southern accent. When I mentioned that, she laughed. "It happens when I'm tired," she said. "Whenever I'm beat, I end up with a Southern drawl. Don't ask me why. Better than mumbling, I suppose. This is one lady who won't be leaving her heart in San Francisco, Jess. Not only was I born here, I intend to die here."

There was an added plus in having Camille as my local publicist and escort. Besides running her own successful public relations business, she moonlighted as a freelance restaurant reviewer for area newspapers and magazines. That proved fortunate for my taste buds, but not for my waistline. I was wined and dined in all the right places—Compton Place Dining Room, Donatello, a barbecued quail flamed tableside at Chinatown's Celadon that was, as they say, to die for, a heavenly *coulibiac* of salmon at Masa's—and then, last night, a legendary California dish, *Celery Victor,* in the St. Francis's elegant Victor's, thirty-two stories up affording breathtaking views of the Golden Gate Bridge and the city's skyline. The restaurant was named for Victor Hirtzler, the French chef who cooked for two decades following the earthquake, and who gave birth to the popular California cuisine now being served in restaurants around the world.

The hotel's spa and health club received a regular visit from me each morning.

This morning was no exception. I'd already ridden ten miles on a stationary bike, worked out on a fancy weight machine, showered, dressed, and was on my second cup of coffee when the first call of the day jarred my reverie. I checked the clock: 6:29. I'd left a six-thirty wake-up call.

"Hello?"

"Good morning, Jessica. Hope I didn't wake you."

What an odd wake-up call.

"Hello?" I said again.

"Jessica. It's Camille."

"Oh, good morning, Camille."

The second line rang. "Camille, hang on a minute."

"Hello?" I said to the second caller.

"Good morning Mrs. Fletcher. This is your wake-up call. It's six-thirty, and fifty-nine degrees outside. Have a wonderful day."

I would have said "thank you" but it was a recorded message. Even the wake-up system was first-rate at the hotel. If I hadn't picked up for the recorded message, a live operator would have called immediately.

I pushed LINE ONE and retrieved Camille. "Camille?"

"Yes, I'm still here. Boy, you're a busy lady this morning."

"Just my wake-up call."

"Oh. Sorry to have woken you."

"You didn't. I've been up since five-thirty. Already put the gym through its paces."

"Good. I'm calling this early because there's been a scheduling change. My mess up. *Today* is the day you'll be visiting the Women's Correctional Facility. Not tomorrow. Sorry. Hope this won't inconvenience you."

"Not at all, although I will need some extra time to get ready for it. What time am I expected?"

"Not until two-thirty. We can skip breakfast if you'd like. Maybe you'd prefer to order room service. We don't have to leave the hotel until one-thirty."

"That will be fine. I was going to do some sight-seeing and shopping this morning, but I'll just put it off until tomorrow. I am free tomorrow morning, right?"

"Absolutely. You have the lunch interview with the book reviewer from the *Examiner*, but that's it."

"Splendid."

"How about meeting downstairs for lunch at noon? That will give you the morning to prepare for the prison visit."

"Sounds good to me. See you then."

The change in schedule actually worked out better for me.

I'd intended to call George Sutherland in London before leaving Cabot Cove to see whether we could meet up in San Francisco, but he beat me to it. He apologized for not having called sooner, explaining that his decision to attend the criminal investigation had been a last-minute one. He'd been working on a difficult case, and wasn't sure he'd be able to break away. But then the prime suspect in the case suddenly confessed, freeing George up to make the trip. He'd be arriving tomorrow night, and was staying at the venerable Mark Hopkins, on Nob Hill. We'd agreed to touch base after his arrival, and to try and find some time together that weekend.

"How far is the prison, Camille?"

Camille and I rode in the back of a white stretch limo that had been waiting in front of the hotel when we finished lunch. It was well stocked with cold bottles of Perrier, as well as a variety of alcoholic beverages. There was a cheese platter, red and white wine, and a state-of-the-art stereo system playing one of my favorite pieces of classical music, Mozart's 40th and 41st "Jupiter" Symphonies.

"What a coincidence," I said as the stirring music filled the limo. "One of my favorites. My favorite version, too. George Szell and the Cleveland Orchestra."

Camille laughed. "We checked," she said. "Your publicist back in New York gave me a list of your favorite music."

"I'm touched—and impressed."

"I just want to make sure your trip is a pleasant one, that's all. Part of the job."

"Well, here's to a job well-done," I said, lifting my Perrier to her Orangina.

Our driver was a rotund, jovial man who had gone out that morning and purchased a copy of my new book, *Blood Relations*. I'd happily signed it to him and his wife before pulling away from the hotel. Now we were on our way across the Golden Gate Bridge.

"I must admit I'm nervous," I said after we'd crossed the span and headed north toward redwood country.

"About today? I am, too."

"Why you?"

"I've never been inside a prison before, Jess. I've been having nightmares ever since arrangements were made for you to talk to the inmates there. I wake up in a cold sweat. In my dream, someone recognizes me as a serial killer the minute we're inside, and they've locked the doors behind us. They toss me in a cell, no trial, no lawyers and I spend the rest of my life there."

I couldn't help but laugh. "That's a terrible dream," I said. "But just a dream—unless . . ."

She, too, laughed. "Unless I *am* a serial killer."

"Are you?"

"I once murdered six mosquitoes in a single night."

"A veritable slaughter," I said.

"Exactly. If I decide not to go in with you, please understand."

"Absolutely not. We do it together, Camille, or not at all."

"If you insist—boss."

"This way, Mrs. Fletcher."

We were greeted at the gate by the prison's warden, a tall, rawboned gentleman with chiseled tan features, flowing silver hair, and wearing a bilge-green suit and black string tie tipped with silver. His name was Paul Pratt.

Warden Pratt led us across a dirt area surrounded by a tall metal fence topped with coils of barbed wire, and into a small wooden building attached to a much larger concrete structure. Two uniformed guards sat behind a scarred desk. They stood at our arrival. "This is Jessica Fletcher," Pratt announced in a loud voice. "And this is Miss Inken."

The guards mumbled a greeting. One of them unlocked a heavy steel door with a key from a chain holding dozens of keys, and stepped back to allow us to enter a long hallway in the main building. We passed beneath harsh fluorescent lights until reaching another metal door. A young guard with severe acne came to attention at the sight of Pratt. "Open up," Pratt ordered. This door was swung open, and we stood at the crossroads of four corridors. I peered down each. They were lined with cells.

Camille and I followed Pratt—closely, I might add—as he headed for what appeared to be still another door at the far end of the corridor that intersected the crossroads from our right. I tried to look straight ahead, but that was impossible. To my left and right were female inmates. Some stood at the doors to their cells, arms hanging out, quizzical, sometimes with angry expressions on their faces. Others lounged on their narrow beds. I'd seen prison movies in which inmates yelled obscenities at visitors, but that didn't happen here. The women looked lethargic, resigned, impassive, almost drugged. It was a sad sight. I glanced at Camille, whose face was set in grim determination, eyes straight ahead, brow tightly knitted.

We reached the door at the end of the hallway. Yet another guard was there to greet us. He started to pull out his keys, but Pratt stopped him. The warden turned to me and said, "I'll be honest with you, Mrs. Fletcher. I wasn't especially keen on your visiting. Frankly, I don't see much good coming from it. These may be women, but they're hard as any man. Some of them are murderers. Bank robbers. No pleasant talk about writing is going to change them. They have criminal minds, and they'll always have criminal minds."

"I really don't know enough to debate it with you, Warden Pratt," I said, forcing a smile. "All I know is that I'm here, and I presume the women I'm to speak with are there, behind that door. My suggestion is that we get on with it."

"I wasn't suggesting we not go through with it," Pratt said, gesturing to the guard to open the door. "Not my call anyway. Damn Department of Corrections in this state has its own agenda. Rehabilitation, they call it. Fat chance of rehabilitating these women."

I thought of Mort Metzger, who probably would agree with Warden Pratt. None of it mattered, however. My earlier apprehension was now replaced with determination to give the best presentation I possibly could to this audience, which represented a first for me. I didn't doubt for a moment that Pratt was right. The women were in prison because they'd committed crimes, and had been convicted by juries of their peers. They were also human beings.

The door swung open to reveal a fairly large room in which two dozen women, wearing drab prison-issue dresses the color of dishwater, sat on black folding metal chairs. There had been obvious attempts at sprucing up the room. The walls were painted seasick institutional green, matching Warden Pratt's suit. The floor was a hard yellow linoleum torn in many places. Two pots of dusty dried flowers sat on a low table, which I assumed was where I'd be sitting. These attempts to provide a more human atmosphere were valiant, but failed. The stark reality of the place negated any such attempts at injecting false humanity into the room. It was prison, pure and simple. It was depressing.

Even if there had been music piped in, and clowns running through the halls, there would be no escaping—literally—the hard fact that this place, not too far from one of the most beautiful cities, was home to mothers, daughters, sisters, and granddaughters. Women. I felt a sudden sense of kinship because, after all, I was one of them.

But I knew that it would be a mistake to lend too sympathetic an ear to their stories. Like a seasoned physician, I would have to put the brakes on my emotions and carry on like a professional. Because the fact was, our bond ended at womanhood. They were prisoners in a state institution. They'd committed crimes. And I was a writer who'd committed no crimes, except perhaps to fail my readers now and then with a misleading red herring, or a character whose voice wasn't true to his personality.

Most important, I was free.

Camille and I stood to one side as Warden Pratt

asked for everyone's attention. Not that he needed to. Most of the women in the room sat quietly, some with arms crossed, their heads cocked in angry defiance of what I had to say before I'd even said it. They looked defeated, which struck me as ironic because I assumed that most of them would never never admit being guilty of the crimes for which they were being punished.

I'd been told that those attending my talk had volunteered to be there. But I began to wonder. Maybe only a few had signed up, and the majority had been pressed into service to fill the room. It really didn't matter. It was my experience that in every group, there would always be one or two who showed genuine interest in what I had to say, and I expected that to hold true even though the audience was made up of prison inmates.

As Pratt read from a piece of paper on which my background and credentials were listed, I took the opportunity to take in each person before me. Most faces were hard, but there were a few who exuded a gentleness, a sad softness. The body language of those women reflected it, too. They sat demurely, legs crossed at the ankles, hands in their laps, their faces open to what they were about to hear. I decided to focus my attention on them, hoping that others would pick up their receptive spirit.

Pratt finished my introduction. Usually, audiences applaud. In this case, only two or three quietly clapped their hands together.

"Good afternoon," I said, coming around in front

of the table and leaning on it. It suddenly occurred to me that the position I'd taken, and my posture, rang of authority, something with which these women had to deal on a daily basis. It wouldn't win me any friends. I spotted an empty chair, pulled it to a spot a few feet in front of the table, and suggested they form a semicircle around me. A few women snickered, but they all adjusted their positions. I took note that they'd arranged themselves into two factions: the hardened cadre, and those women whose faces were not quite so defiant.

"That's better," I said. "Much less formal. And a perfect segue into what I am about to discuss with you today. I imagine you were told I'd be *talking* to you. But I much prefer the word *discuss*, because I encourage each of you to talk as much as I do. To exchange thoughts with me. If you do, you'll help save my voice, and I think you'll find it a more interesting hour."

The twelve angry women on one side of the circle stared at me, their faces hardened and weather-beaten, although the pallor of their skin said they haven't seen the sun very much.

I continued: "Of course, if you choose not to talk, and to just listen, that's certainly your right and choice." I turned to the "softer" side of the circle. "As you probably already know, I am a writer. I write mystery books." I deliberately chose not to use the word *murder*.

"I've written more books than I can remember— some I choose not to remember. The reason I'm here today is to share with you what I know about writing, and the positive effect it can have on a person's life." I paused. One young woman with frizzy brown hair smiled at me. I smiled back. "Let me begin by asking all of you if you write in a journal, or keep a daily diary."

Encouragingly, several hands rose from women on both sides of the semicircle.

"Good. Then, I assume you know the benefits of doing it. Writing down our thoughts is a healthy and therapeutic way of dealing with our emotions. Sometimes, by writing, we discover emotions we didn't even know existed until we see them in black and white."

There were a few nods of recognition.

"Would anyone care to tell those who don't keep a journal why they might enjoy doing so?"

Several of the women spoke at once. I was relieved. Let them do the talking. I'll moderate.

"I write every day," said a middle-aged black woman, expressionless. "I write for my children. In a way I'm talking to them through my writing. Sometimes I even leave room on the page for them, like we're really talking. I leave blanks for their answers and thoughts." She took a long, deep breath before continuing. "Fifteen minutes through that glass window ain't enough. So I spend hours every day *talking* to them on paper."

"That's a lovely reason to write," I said, swallowing against a lump in my throat.

"I'd write if I could," said another member of the

group. I judged her to be younger than what her appearance said. The lines on her face were as deep as the San Andres fault. "But I don't know how to write," she said. "I mean, I can write and read, but I'm not good at it."

"That's the beauty of a journal," I interrupted. "You don't have to be *good* at it. It's for *your* eyes only. At times in my life, when I've kept a journal— and I must admit I don't have the time to do it every day—I can barely read my handwriting, especially when I've written an entry late at night. But it doesn't matter. Writing in a journal involves a process that frees your mind, and allows you to get in touch with your feelings. It is for you and no one else. In a sense, a journal is the enabler. Do you know what that means? It means it enables you to expose yourself. It doesn't matter if it's grammatically correct, or if words are misspelled. The idea is to just write, and then leave it alone."

"It matters to me!"

The loud voice belonged to a thick-set woman with close-cropped black hair. I'd originally pegged her as one of the more reserved ones, everything being relative, of course.

"What matters to you?" I asked.

Her voice continuing to rise: "When I get out of this hole, I want to *publish* my journal. Let the world know how we live in here. They treat us like dogs. No. Dogs have it better."

"Maybe that's a possibility," I said. "There have

been books written before by prisoners. If your journal is good, then I think—"

"You gave me a good idea. I'll write it, and you can give it to your publisher. Tell him to publish it. Tell him—"

"It isn't quite that easy," I said. "I'm really not talking about publishing the journals and diaries you write. I want you to think of them as self-therapy. As a way to vent your feelings, and to come to grips with things inside you that might have led you to do the things that brought you here."

She mumbled a few four-letter words under her breath, folded her arms tightly across her chest, and glared at me. I decided to try and pull her back into the group. "How long have you been keeping your diary?" I asked.

She shrugged. "I'm going to start writing tonight," she said. "I have five years to go in this dump."

"Plenty of time to write a very good—and long— diary," I said.

"Don't hold your breath, lady," a young—too young—black woman sitting next to her said to me. "She spends so much time bitchin', she got no time to write." Everyone laughed, and the women continued to banter back and forth between themselves. I was happy to see it. They might have lost their freedom, but evidently hadn't lost their sense of humor.

After a few minutes, I decided it was time to intervene. "Let's get back on track, shall we?" The noise didn't let up. "Ladies, can we quiet things down a little, please?" The warden was poised to step in but I waved him away with a shake of my head.

The talking finally stopped. "Thank you. I've brought some materials with me I'd like to hand out. The first page you'll get is a copy of a typical journal entry. But remember, this is merely a sample. As we've already said, a journal entry is a *completely* private and personal thing. There is no right or wrong way to write an entry. I photocopied this just to show you one possible way you *might* go about doing it."

"Mrs. Fletcher?"

I looked up from the pile of papers and into the eyes of a thirtyish woman, with shoulder-length silver-blond hair that gleamed from a recent shampooing. Her hand was raised. Funny, I thought, but I hadn't noticed her before. Some people are that way. They just seem to blend into the background.

"Yes, dear?" I said, wishing I hadn't used such a patronizing word. As I looked at her, I realized how strikingly beautiful she was despite a lack of makeup. She had model's features—small, finely etched nose, thick, healthy hair, and impressive cheekbones. Most noticeable, however, were her large, expressive green eyes. There was a childlike innocence to them. There was also intelligence.

"Mrs. Fletcher," she said in a husky, hushed voice. "May I change subjects for a minute?"

"Of course."

"I'd like to ask you a question about your murder mystery writing."

"All right. We can discuss anything you'd like."

"I've read most of your books, Mrs. Fletcher. At the end, the murderer is always found, convicted, and jailed. But have you ever written a book in which the clues didn't add up? Where the character you identify as the murderer couldn't have done it?"

The room was silent. A few feet shuffled; the hum of a motorized clock on the wall was audible for the first time.

I wasn't sure where her question would lead, or was intended to lead. Obviously, it wasn't one of your classic what-if questions that a child might ask. Nor was it one that could be answered without thought.

She locked those big green eyes on mine and waited for my reply. I looked back at Camille, who sat at the table behind me. She smiled. I again looked at the women in my audience. Forty-eight eyes peered back at me.

"I must confess," I began, "that there are certain times when even I, as the author of a crime novel, question whether the clues add up and support my choice of murderer. What always concerns me is whether the reader will have found a piece of evidence that doesn't link the murderer to the crime. Or dictates that someone else must have done it. *Should* have done it."

The woman nodded. "Thank you, Mrs. Fletcher," she said.

"Jessica, you did splendidly. Congratulations."

"Thank you, Camille. You're very kind. It was

tougher than I thought it would be. Emotionally, I mean. It's such a sad place, and I pity those women. Of course, I'm dealing from a handicap. I'm sure many of the crimes that put them behind bars were horrible."

We were in the white limo heading back to the city. I felt a fulfilling sense of accomplishment. Once we'd gotten past the woman's question about murderers in my books, we focused for the rest of the hour on writing and keeping a journal. The group, for the most part, turned out to be enthusiastic participants. I relaxed as we went along. The only nervous person in the room seemed to be Warden Pratt. Maybe "nervous" isn't the word. He was more annoyed than nervous, for reasons of his own. I think he was glad to escort us from the prison and see us gone. I suppose I shouldn't be overly harsh in judging him. Spending one's working days in such a depressing environment certainly must take its toll.

"You, know, Jessica, I was really moved by the whole experience," Camille said. "I've always thought that once you're in prison, what's the point of doing anything with your life? Me? I think I'd just curl up and die. But these women, at least many of them, still have life in them, and want to do something with themselves."

"I hope I inspired at least one of them to write her story," I said. "If only to help come to terms with her life."

The music for our drive back to the hotel was

another favorite of mine, Beethoven string quartets written toward the end of his life, and representing some of his finest work. I sat back, watched the scenery glide by the window, and thought back to the young blond woman who'd asked the question about whether I'd ever falsely accused a character of murder in one of my books. Did she feel she'd been imprisoned for a crime she hadn't committed? Probably. I shuddered as I contemplated being sentenced to prison for something I hadn't done. It undoubtedly happens. You see headlines all the time: MAN WHO SPENT SEVEN YEARS IN JAIL IS SET FREE; TRUE KILLER CONFESSES.

I wished I'd gotten her name and learned more about her. What was the crime for which she'd been convicted? Was it murder?

"Jessica?" Camille said as we pulled up in front of the St. Francis.

"I'm still here," I said, laughing. "Just daydreaming."

"Like a drink?" Camille asked.

"Sounds heavenly," I said. "But I'd like to enjoy it while soaking in a tub of hot water. Mind?"

"Of course not. You were terrific today. In fact, of all the authors I've handled, you are *the* class act."

"That's very kind of you," I said.

"You may not think so when I admit another scheduling mistake on my part."

I raised my eyebrows.

"A photo shoot right after breakfast. Nine o'clock.

Right here at the hotel. Promise it won't take more than a half hour."

"Okay," I said.

"Then the lunch interview, and that's it."

"Until you remember something else."

Her brow furrowed.

"Just kidding," I said. "Have a wonderful evening." I kissed her on the cheek. The driver opened the door. I dragged my heavy black bag behind me (it seemed a lot heavier than when I'd left the hotel earlier in the day), wished him a pleasant evening, and entered the busy lobby.

A moment ago, I'd wanted to soak in a tub and sip white wine. But the superb weather changed my mind. I thought of the heat wave I'd left back in Maine, which hadn't broken, according to a phone call from Seth. Here, in San Francisco, there was a misty breeze that had cooled and dampened my skin as I left the climate-controlled limo. Refreshing. Invigorating. It was too magnificent a night to spend sitting inside a hotel room, even a spectacular suite like the Windsor.

I returned to the street. "I'd like a cab, please," I told the elegantly uniformed doorman. He blew his whistle, and a cab instantly pulled to the curb. I debated for a moment going back inside to drop off my heavy black bag. But the cab was there, and the doorman had opened its door. "Here you are, lovely lady," he said. "Enjoy your evening."

"Thank you," I said. "I know I will."

* * *

"A very dry martini, straight up," I told the waitress as I settled at a window table in the Mark Hopkins's Top of the Mark cocktail lounge. I don't drink martinis as a rule. Only on the most special of occasions. And I considered this one of them. The Top of the Mark has meaning for me as few other places in the world have. I'm not alone, of course. During World War II, thousands of people looked out the windows at troop ships sailing beneath the fabled Golden Gate Bridge, returning triumphantly from war in the South Pacific.

The Top of the Mark is considered by many to *define* San Francisco. They get no argument from me.

As I watched a cocoon of fog swallow the Golden Gate, and thought of George Sutherland arriving the next night, my waitress returned with my drink. She also had a copy of the book I was promoting, *Blood Relations*.

"Excuse me, Mrs. Fletcher. I hope you don't think this is pushy of me, but I knew you were in town and figured that maybe—well, I bought your book and kept it here just in case you happened to come by." A wide smile lit up her face. "And here you are."

"Yes. Here I am."

"Would you be good enough to autograph it for me?"

"Of course." She handed me the book, and the ballpoint pen she carried. I opened the book. "Who shall I sign it to?"

"Frances."

"Okay, Frances." I started to write, but the pen had run dry.

"I'll get another," she said.

"No need," I said. "I have a dozen of them in my bag."

I unzipped the bag and pulled it up onto my lap, surprised again at its weight. I fumbled in its recesses for one of the Flair pens I always carry for just such occasions. "What's this?" I asked myself. There was a hefty black leather-bound book. It wasn't mine. I'd never seen it before. Whose was it? How did it get there?

I started to remove it but remembered Frances standing next to me. I fished out a pen and signed her book: *"To Frances. I have a favorite aunt named Frances. Let's hope you and I aren't 'blood relations' or we may never meet again. Best, Jessica Fletcher."*

I handed her the book, saying, "You'll understand why I wrote what I did after you finish it."

Blood Relations turned out to be one of my more graphic novels. It hinged on the mysterious deaths of a half-dozen blood relatives, some of whom had never even met each other before. The reviews have been kind, although one did point out the uncharacteristically gory details in the novel—uncharacteristic for this writer, at least. The reviewer wrote: *"Blood is to* Blood Relations *what showers are to* Psycho. *You'll never feel the same about blood again—relatively speaking."*

I supposed he couldn't resist the pun at the end, although I wish he had.

Frances, the waitress, offered to buy me a drink, but I graciously declined. I'd barely touched my martini, and two were out of the question. I looked out the window. The fog had now enveloped the city itself; visibility appeared to be zero. It was a moody atmosphere, the stuff good British mystery movies are made of. Inside the Top of the Mark, it was cozy and secure. I ordered an appetizer of a sampling of cheeses and fruits, took a sip of my martini, took out the unfamiliar, imposing black notebook from my bag, and began to read.

November 1. My first day in prison. As they say, the first day of the rest of my life. I want to scream, "I didn't do it." I want to tell the other inmates, the guards, everyone I see. "I'm not like you. I didn't do it. I don't know who killed my husband but I didn't." I guess I'm supposed to believe that God knows I didn't kill Mark. But given the lack of my religious faith, I guess Santa Claus knows I didn't do it either. I have just two questions as I begin my days and nights here in Hell— How did I get here, and how do I get out? Goodnight.

I pondered which of the female inmates present at my presentation had surreptitiously placed the journal in my bag. I looked everywhere for a name but couldn't find one.

As I took another sip of my martini, my thoughts

went back to the pretty woman with blond hair who'd asked the question about a convicted murderer's innocence. For some reason, I was certain the diary belonged to her. But how, when did she manage to slip it into my bag? Of course. During the brief break when I went to the bathroom. I'd left my bag behind. Camille was there, but was busy talking. I continued reading.

I have one goal while spending my time here, and that is to once again feel the burning desire to write books for children. Writing for children is the one passion in my life. I miss it so. But the only way I will be able to do that is to be emancipated from here. In order to write for children, one has to always be aware of their innocence, and be careful not to disturb it in any way. A child's innocence is precious and vulnerable. Being forced to spend my days and nights here is a stark contradiction. I was robbed of my innocence when I was a child. Now I've been robbed of it again. I am innocent of this crime. I remember as a child feeling the same overwhelming emotion—to scream to someone, anyone, to remind them of my innocence, and of my right to live my life as that innocent being.

Kimberly Steffer!

Of course. The inmate who'd written this journal was Kimberly Steffer, convicted of having murdered her husband, Mark Steffer. It had happened in California, San Francisco. She was a noted author of children's books. I was willing to bet that it was

Kimberly who'd asked me that afternoon about wrongly convicted murder suspects.

I thought back to the book that my friend Neil had written, *Scarlet Sins*. I wished I'd read it, at least that chapter, on the plane. I certainly would the minute I returned to my room at the St. Francis. The diary, too. It looked like I was in for a long evening of reading. I paid my check, cabbed back to the hotel, ordered up room service, ate, filled the tub with hot water and a bath gel, sunk into the sea of luxurious bubbles, and propped open Neil's book and started.

Chapter Four

"Nice story, Bill. And factually correct. I always appreciate accuracy, especially when it's about me."

I was sitting in the office of Bill Hudson, the *San Francisco Chronicle*'s features editor. He'd interviewed me, and written a story that had run in Wednesday's paper. I'm always on my guard when being interviewed. Too often, reporters put words in my mouth in order to make their piece say what they *want* it to say, which is not necessarily synonymous with what I'd actually said. Happily, that hadn't been the case with Hudson's article.

"Coming from you, Jessica, I consider it quite a compliment," Hudson said. "Glad you liked it. To tell you the truth, though, when you called yesterday to say you wanted to meet with me, I was worried. I thought you had a problem with the article."

"Oh, no. Hardly," I said. "You worried over nothing."

Hudson was an average-looking fellow, about thirty-eight years old, medium height, slender build, wavy brown hair, and muddy brown eyes. Brown slacks, brown tie, and a brown tweed jacket completed his earth-tone image.

His writing, however, was above average. He had a lively style that was visual and anecdotal. I could see why he'd risen quickly at the *Chronicle,* having become features editor in two short years.

"You know, Jessica, I was thinking after the interview that you should do your life story. Not only are you this country's preeminent writer of murder mysteries, you've ended up solving your share."

"Just a matter of being in the wrong place at the wrong time," I said.

"Very modest. But there's a lot more to your life than that. It could be fascinating, to say nothing of inspiring for many people, especially writers. Like *this* writer."

I think I blushed.

"Hey," he said, startling me with his sudden enthusiasm. "Since you like the piece I wrote about you so much, keep me in mind if you're looking for a collaborator on your autobiography. Maybe I could be your Boswell."

"But your name is Hudson."

"I'll change it. So, to what do I owe this honor of a second meeting with you?"

Because the walls of his small cubicle didn't reach all the way to the ceiling, I spoke softly. "I'm interested in a murder case that took place in San Francisco a couple of years ago. Kimberly Steffer. She was accused and convicted of killing her husband, Mark. She's doing her time in the Women's Correctional Facility."

He nodded in recognition, at the same time struggling with a balky top on his styrofoam coffee cup. "Sure," he said. "Big case here. Got lots of media play. I didn't cover it, but half the staff got involved at one time or another. How 'bout we go to the morgue and see what we can find?"

I followed him from the cubicle and down a narrow hall lined with similar spaces until we reached the paper's "morgue," that important function of any newspaper or magazine in which a complete record of everything appearing in the publication is catalogued and filed. It was a small, crowded room this morning. Bill gestured for me to take a seat next to him in front of a computer. He punched up the name STEFFER, KIMBERLY. "Here we go," he said. "I'll leave you to read the articles. Just pull up each of the files you want to look at by placing the cursor in front of the file name, and press ENTER. Pretty basic stuff."

I hoped so. While making the switch from writing on a manual typewriter to writing on a computer, I practically had to enlist in a Twelve Step program. After what seemed to be an eternity of agonizing days and countless mistakes, I reached a point where I'm now able to log on, write, edit, and store. But that's about it.

But Hudson's instructions were easy enough. I successfully pulled up the first file.

Kimberly Steffer, wife of restaurateur Mark Steffer, who was found shot to death in his car earlier this week, has been arrested and charged in that murder. Mrs. Steffer, who holds dual citizenship in the United States and the United Kingdom, was arrested at her home in Sausalito late last night.

I pulled up several more files; each story had been written by a reporter named Bobby McCormick. I looked around the morgue in search of Bill Hudson, who was planted in front of another computer screen. "Bill," I said.

"Over here," he said. "Finding what you need?"

"Yes. Is a reporter named Bobby McCormick still with the paper?"

"I might be in a morgue, but I ain't dead yet" came a voice from over my left shoulder. I turned to face a tall, grinning bear of a man with a day's growth of beard. His gray-and-brown hair was sparse on top but long on the sides, pulled back into a ponytail secured by a red-and-gold band. He wore chino pants, sneakers sans socks, a plaid button-down shirt open at the neck, and a stained yellow tie pulled down into a tiny, tight knot. "Bobby McCormick," he said. "At your service." He extended his hand.

"Behave yourself, Bobby," Hudson said, draping an arm easily over his colleague's shoulder. "This is Jessica Fletcher. *The* Jessica Fletcher."

"Of course it is," said McCormick. "Hardly an unfamiliar face, especially if you read stories in the

Chronicle by Bill Hudson. I won't say I've read all
your books, but a good number of them. Pleasure
meeting you, Mrs. Fletcher."

"The feeling is mutual," I said. "The reason I
asked if you were still with the paper is that I see
you covered the Kimberly Steffer trial extensively."

"Sure did. And I wouldn't be surprised if I ended
up covering another Kimberly Steffer trial."

"Really? I'd be interested in knowing why. Would
you spend a couple of minutes talking with me
about the Steffer case? I'm—well, I'm very interested in it."

"Be my pleasure."

"Wonderful," I said. I liked Bobby McCormick.
He was obviously a character, a throwback to the
image of a beat reporter from another era.

"Give me a couple of minutes?" he said. "Just
have to finish up something here."

"Of course. Take your time."

"Come on," said Bill Hudson. "I'll take you to
Bobby's office." He said to McCormick, "Can we
get in it this morning?"

"If you're lucky."

"Bobby's office is not what you'd call an oasis of
neatness and order," Hudson said as he led me from
the morgue. "But at least he has a real office, not
one of the cubicles. That's what happens when you
become a living legend like Bobby. He's been the
crime reporter here for twenty years, maybe more.
He's the best. Crime's a tough beat."

*   *   *

Bobby's office reminded me of a bachelor's pad. Did he live as well as work there? It was chockablock with books, magazines, yellow copy paper, and empty boxes. Clothing was tossed in every corner, and a dozen dirty coffee cups perched precariously on stacks of old newspapers. Tasteless calendars of naked women hung on the walls; some were four years old. The date, not the models. A life-size poster of John Lennon and the Beatles took up most of one wall. Framed photos and plaques dominated another. A computer screen peeked out from where it was partially buried beneath some shirts.

My nose started to itch; a major sneeze was in the offing. I figured the room hadn't been dusted for the duration of McCormick's tenure at the paper.

Bill Hudson blessed me, and laughed. "I have an interview to do in a couple of minutes. Make yourself at home, if that's possible. Stop by my cubicle on your way out."

"Shall do. And thanks for everything."

I didn't sit because there was no place to sit, except for McCormick's chair behind the desk. The only other chair in the room was piled high with record albums. I perused the top LPs. All rock 'n' roll from another time.

I was in the process of reading plaques on the wall, mostly awards McCormick had garnered from area press associations, when he entered the office. "Well, Mrs. Fletcher, welcome to McCormick's lair. Ask me to find anything. There's a place for everything in here, including its occupant." He struggled past debris to reach his chair and fell heavily into it. Then he slung his large feet up onto the desk, realized I had no place to sit, came back around to where I stood, removed the albums from the visitor's chair and put them on the floor. Finally, he gestured for me to take the seat. He made his way back to his chair, got his feet up on the desk again, and smiled. "So, have you come here to steal some good plot ideas? The world's getting weirder and weirder. Don't need fiction anymore, do we? It's got to the point where a fiction writer's imagination can't hold a goddamn candle to real life."

"Right you are," I said, shaking my head. "It makes my job that much tougher. Yours, too, I imagine."

"Yeah, it does. When I first came here, I covered what I call 'monotonous murder.' Same story, different cast of characters. Now the stuff I see turns even my stomach. And I've got a stomach made of steel, Mrs. Fletcher. Chili peppers go down easy and stay that way. Never took a Tum in my life. But the way people go around killing other people these days churns me up now and then. Some of it's not even fit for a family newspaper, but readers are different these days, too. Can't get enough blood and guts it seems. Weirdness on all sides. Surrounded by it."

I listened patiently as he continued his take on the deterioration of the human condition.

"But not up to me to judge anybody, huh, Mrs. Fletcher? I have a job to do. I do it. They want gore,

I give 'em gore. Factual gore. Not like the gore you make up in your books." He let out a thunderous laugh, ending with a coughing spasm which, along with a massive filled-to-the-brim ashtray, testified to a two-pack-a-day smoking habit. Probably why he's got his own office, I thought. The air in the room was stale and odorous. The newsroom was undoubtedly a smoke-free zone. Same with the cubicles lined up next to each other, with their open tops that allow smoke to drift from one to the other. Unpleasant for nonsmokers.

"Move over, Stephen King," McCormick continued. "Move over, Jessica Fletcher. Here comes *real* life." He lit a cigarette, coughed, and spread his hands out in a welcoming gesture. "So, where do we begin?" he asked, eyeing several "While You Were Out" memos.

"What did you mean when you said you wouldn't be surprised to be covering another Kimberly Steffer trial?"

He replied without looking up, "I said that, Mrs. Fletcher, because I don't think Kimberly Steffer is guilty."

"Really?"

"That's right. Nothing ever really linked her to the crime except a bunch of goddamn coincidences. In my opinion, if you ask me—and it looks like you are—I think she was framed. Set up. Her attorney tried to get that across to the jury but fell flat on his smug face. They never found the gun. They found her fingerprints in the car, but it was her

56

husband's car, for crying out loud. Why wouldn't her fingerprints be in there? Her biggest mistake was going to the mall the day he was found murdered. And that could have been coincidental. But they found receipts in her purse that showed she'd been there that day, and the jury latched on to it because the prosecutor made damn sure they did."

Still not looking at me, he continued.

"Yeah, sure, the cabdriver who allegedly picked up a woman fitting Steffer's description at the mall that day made points for the prosecution. But hell, he wore glasses thick as Coke bottles. And the testimony from other so-called prosecution witnesses was weak. Who were they?" He glanced at me. I shrugged. "I'll tell you who they were. Her husband's ex-wife, and the ex-wife's best friend. You look up the word 'biased' in any dictionary, you see pictures of those witnesses."

I laughed.

"Not funny."

"I—"

He lit up another cigarette. I now viewed him through a blue smoky haze. "Unfortunately, the jury bought it," he said. "The prosecuting attorney did a hell of a good job pinning the rap on Kimberly Steffer. Her attorney was a pompous dunce. She didn't have a chance."

"Mr. McCormick, is—"

"Call me Bobby. Yeah, yeah, I know. I'm too old to be called Bobby. But one look at me, and you know I'm not a 'Robert.' 'Bob' sounds dumb to me, like some dork in a bad radio commercial. So it's always been Bobby."

"All right. Bobby it is. Bobby, is Kimberly Steffer currently at the Women's Correctional Facility?"

"Yup. She'll be there a long time unless she can come up with some hot-shot attorney with brains this time around to get her another trial. So, Mrs. Fletcher, how come you're interested in this case?"

"Jessica," I said. "Or, Jess."

"Right. So? What's with the interest in Kimberly Steffer?"

"I was at the Women's Correctional Facility yesterday. I spoke to some of the inmates about writing. I think one of the women in the audience was Kimberly Steffer. At least I assume it was her. She asked some interesting questions. I've been thinking about her ever since. There's a quality to her—if it was Kimberly Steffer—that's appealing." I didn't intend to tell McCormick, or anyone else for that matter, about the diary she'd planted in my bag. He'd want to see it, but it would be an act of betrayal on my part to share it with anyone—unless, of course, there was a compelling reason, a reason that would help Steffer.

"What's she look like these days?" he asked.

"Silver-blond hair cut smartly to the shoulders, almond-shaped face, elegant features, soft eyes. Sad eyes. Intelligent eyes."

"Sounds like she's riding it out okay."

"I'm not sure I'd say that, Bobby."

He shrugged, torched another cigarette into action, adding to the room's noxious smog. My eyes had begun to sting. "Mind if I smoke?" he asked.

"Oh, no, of course not."

"Want one?" He extended the pack to me.

"No, thanks. Too early for me. You say Kimberly Steffer was framed. Who framed her?" I coughed, and rubbed my eyes.

"Wish I knew," he answered. "I have my ideas, but that's all they are. *My* ideas. Which don't mean a damn thing in court. How about you, Jessica? Got any ideas about who might have framed Kimberly Steffer?"

"No. I'm just beginning to learn about the case. Maybe after I've had a chance to read up more on it, I'll come to some conclusions. With a little help from those in-the-know. Like a Bobby McCormick."

"I'm available anytime, Jessica. Things are slow this week. Just your run-of-the-mill dopers whacking each other. I like to see that. Saves lots of tax dollars. I keep hoping there'll be another case like the Steffer one. Something to get my teeth into."

"You mentioned Kimberly had been at a mall. Why is that significant?"

"That's where her husband's restaurant is located. He was found in his car around back. Kimberly claimed she wasn't at the mall that day. But witnesses—especially that vision-impaired cabdriver—said otherwise."

"I see." I stood and extended my hand across the desk. He took it in his large paw and slowly pushed himself up from his chair. "You know what I think?" he said.

"What?"

"I think you're about to find yourself a *cause* in Kimberly Steffer. I think you might end up the best thing that's ever happened to her. And if that's the case, I'd like to tag along for the ride."

"Count on it," I said. "Have you ever thought of installing some sort of exhaust system in here?"

"No need. I have a window. Just can't get it open. Painted shut. Keep in touch, Jessica."

"You can count on that, too."

Chapter Five

"Hello, Kimberly."

Even through the Plexiglas window between us functioning as an airbrush of sorts, Kimberly's natural beauty didn't need its softening quality. She looked even more beautiful than when I'd first seen her the day of my talk. Her skin was flawless; no line or crease marred it. Her hair had the same radiant shine. But the sadness was still there in her eyes, pleading for understanding. Which I was at the Woman's Correctional Facility to give.

Her smile was small. "Hello," she said.

"I didn't expect to be here again," I said.

"I didn't expect to see you again, either," she said.

"But I assume you *wanted* to see me again."

"Yes, I did."

"The book in my bag. It is yours?"

Kimberly looked down at her lap and nodded.

"It's beautifully written," I said. "You're an excellent writer. I bought two of your children's books. They're wonderful."

Tears welled up in the corners of her eyes. Her "thank you" was barely audible.

"Kimberly," I said, getting as close to the partition as possible, "I'd like to help you. I find your story compelling. And you're not the only one who believes in your innocence."

Her eyes widened. "Really?"

"Really. Look. Ms. Steffer, I don't know if I can help you. But maybe you can help me. Where should I begin?"

"Begin?"

"To help establish your innocence."

"You will?"

"Where do I start?"

She replied without hesitation. "Call Ellie. She's my stepdaughter. The daughter of Mark's first wife, Joan. I think Ellie knows what really happened to Mark."

"She lives with her mother now?"

"No. She lives with her godmother, Nancy Antonio, Joan's best friend. Ellie was a rebellious teenager, especially after her parents' divorce. She ran away. The only way she was coaxed back was a promise that she wouldn't have to live with her mother. She wanted to live with Nancy. Strange— at least it is to me—that Nancy and Joan are still best of friends. Last I heard, anyway. I think Joan was relieved, actually, to be rid of Ellie on a daily basis. She resented the responsibility of being tied down by a youngster. Let me put it this way. Joan would never win the PTA award as mother of the year."

"Where do Ellie and Ms. Antonio live?"

"I heard they moved, but I believe they're still in the Bay Area."

"Kimberly. Do you know who killed Mark?"

Her eyes locked on mine. The tears were gone. "No," she said. "I wish I did."

We fell silent, each occupied with our own thoughts. I knew I'd have to be leaving soon. The guard kept glancing at a giant clock hanging over our heads. Our visit was almost up.

"Mrs. Fletcher, Mark had a partner in the restaurant he owned. Robert Frederickson. I never trusted Bob from the day I met him. With Mark's death, Bob ended up owning the restaurant."

"What's it called?" I asked.

"It's called, 'What's To Eat?' It's in Sausalito."

"You say you didn't trust your husband's partner. But do you think he was capable of murdering your husband?"

"In my opinion, Bob Frederickson is capable of anything. Including murder if it helps him get what he wants."

"Was he considered a suspect? Did the police question him?"

"Sure. But he had an alibi."

"All right," I said. "There's your stepdaughter, Ellie, to contact. And I think a meal at What's To Eat? is also in order." The guard used a hand gesture to inform me it was time to leave. "I'll be back, Kimberly. In the meantime, don't lose faith."

"I didn't have much faith after my conviction, but I do now that someone like you has taken an interest."

"I'll do what I can. I'd like to keep your diary for a while. I have it with me, and if you'd rather I—"

"Keep it as long as you like, Mrs. Fletcher. I've started another."

"Good. I'll be in touch."

She shrugged her shoulders and smiled as the guard waved her toward a door leading back to the cell blocks. Her head was down as she left the room, but I was certain her mood was elevated.

And I had a lot of work to do.

What's to Eat? fell into the category of "family restaurant." More accurately, it spoke to the dining needs of children. The exterior walls were painted bright red, yellow, and blue. The signage was written with some of the letters backward, obviously inspired by Toys 'R' Us. An enormous playground with state-of-the-art equipment spread out behind the restaurant and around one side. The parking lot in front could accommodate at least a hundred cars, and virtually every spot was filled by the time my cabdriver dropped me at the canopied entrance.

I entered and immediately felt out of place. The vast expanse of the main dining room was filled with young mothers and their even younger children. No business lunches at What's to Eat? I thought as a hostess, barely out of childhood herself and wearing what appeared to be Judy Garland's dress from *The Wizard of Oz*, greeted me with startling enthusiasm. "Hi," she bubbled. "How many?" She had to yell over the din of a hundred children, made worse by a tin ceiling that caught every decibel, magnified it, and tossed it back at the customers' ears.

"Just me," I said loudly. "And something as far away as possible from that." I pointed to a round table of a dozen kids and their mothers. Colorful balloons on long, ribbon tethers reached for the ceiling. A pile of wrapped presents cluttered the floor. A birthday party.

"Sure," said the hostess. She pronounced it the way comedians always make fun of the way California's "Valley Girls" talk. I smiled and followed her as she bounced across the main room to a blessedly quiet, all things being relative, back room that was tastefully decorated in more subdued pastels. I silently pledged to generously tip her on my way out for sensing that I was not interested in singing "Happy Birthday" to anyone.

"Here you go," she said, pulling out a wooden chair with a pig's head carved into its back. "Have you ever dined with us before?"

"No."

"Well, remember to ask your waitress when she comes to the table, 'What's to Eat?'"

I laughed. "And if I don't?"

"You have to go to your room without dinner."

Unsure of whether I'd taken her seriously and was offended, she quickly added, "Just kidding."

"Yes, I was sure you were."

The moment the hostess disappeared, an "Annie" look-a-like with a gingham apron wrapped around her small frame appeared at the table. Her name tag read MOM. "Hello," she said, "and welcome. How are you today?"

"Very well, thank you."

We looked at each other. She held a large menu in her hands. "Oops," I said. "Almost forgot. What's to eat?"

She handed me the menu and said she'd be back for my order.

I seriously considered ordering a peanut butter and jelly sandwich, which would have been a nice departure from the heavy, elegant foods I'd been indulging in for the past week. The last time I'd ordered peanut butter and jelly, the waitress in the Boston luncheonette told me that it was only offered on the children's menu. Since I wasn't a child, I couldn't have one. Needless to say, I never returned to that restaurant.

I chose a tuna sandwich on whole wheat, and an iced tea. When it was served, I asked the waitress if Mr. Frederickson was in. She said he was, and offered to get him. "Who shall I say wants to see him?"

"Mrs. Fletcher."

A few minutes later, a handsome, forty-something man headed my way. "Hello. I'm Robert Frederickson," he said when he reached the table. He was tall and reed-thin, allowing an obviously expensive gray pinstripe suit to fall nicely on his frame. Every black hair was in place. His tan was a deep copper. "What can I do for you?" he asked, the tan accentuating the whiteness of his teeth.

It was a reasonable question. Fortunately, I'd decided during lunch the approach I'd take if I got to meet him.

"Pleased to meet you, Mr. Frederickson. My name is Jessica Fletcher. You have a wonderful place here. I wish I'd brought along someone three-quarters my age so that I could taste some of the more whimsical items. Like the 'Barney the Purple Dinosaur Dessert Sandwich.' I'm afraid I'd feel silly ordering it for myself."

Frederickson laughed. "No need to feel silly in this restaurant, Mrs. Fletcher. That's what What's to Eat? is all about. Is that why you wanted to see me? If so, I give you permission to indulge yourself in the Barney sandwich, the Mickey Mouse sundae, even the Mr. Rogers lollipop."

I laughed along with him. "That's very kind of you. I'll no longer hesitate to let the child in me out. But that really isn't why I wanted to meet the owner. The fact is, I'm a mystery book writer. For adults. But my agent, and my publisher, have suggested I begin a series of murder mysteries for younger people. Children's mysteries. I'm about to start the outline for the first book in the series and, frankly, came here today because I'd heard a great deal about What's to Eat? I wanted to scope it out as a place to set a possible scene. I always enjoy weaving real places into my books."

Frederickson arched his back like a cat as he extended his arms in front of him, laced his fingers together and stretched, then used both hands to pat hairs on his head that weren't out of place. "A scene?"

"Yes. I figured kids would better enjoy reading a murder mystery novel if they were familiar with the settings."

"Will you excuse me, Mrs. Fletcher? I'll be right back."

He returned, a dazzling smile painted on his handsome face. "You'll have to forgive me, Mrs. Fletcher," he said. "I didn't catch your name at first, or at least didn't connect it with the famous person you are. You are *the* Jessica Fletcher, aren't you?"

I nodded.

"Of course you are. Mind if I sit down?"

"Please."

When he was seated, and had carefully crossed his legs and checked the creases in his trousers by running thumb and forefinger down them, he said, "Mrs. Fletcher, I am truly flattered that you would consider setting a scene in What's to Eat?. I mean, who wouldn't be flattered? But I'm afraid—"

"Of what?" I asked sweetly.

"Of what? Oh, no. I'm not afraid—of something. What I mean is, it's really not something we'd be interested in becoming involved with. At least not at this time. A rain check? In one of your future books?"

"I'm disappointed to hear that, Mr. Frederickson. I'm quite impressed with your restaurant and was excited about the possibilities of using it in my book."

"I am sorry, Mrs. Fletcher. Maybe another time. By the way, could I ask a favor of you?"

"Favor?"

"A picture of you with me? I have a number of celebrity pictures in my den at home."

"Do you?"

"Yes. Mostly sports figures when they come here to promote the restaurant. Just take a minute."

I didn't agree. But while I waited for the check, he disappeared, returning with a young man carrying a camera.

"I was waiting for a check," I said.

"No check, Mrs. Fletcher. On me."

The three of us walked through the main dining room, which by now had quieted down, and stepped outside. "Right over there," Frederickson said. "By the sign."

"All right," I said. I posed next to him as the young man clicked off a few shots.

"Thanks, Mrs. Fletcher. Maybe when it's developed, you'll sign one to me."

"I don't think I'll have a chance to do that," I said.

"Tell me where you're staying. I'll put a rush on these and personally deliver them to you tomorrow. You can sign it then. I like them when they're signed. Makes them seem more personal. Don't you agree?"

"Thanks for lunch."

"You have a car?"

"No. And I forgot to call for a cab."

"Petey, get your car and drive Mrs. Fletcher back to San Francisco. Drop off the film at a one-hour place. Wait around until it's ready."

I protested, but Frederickson insisted. He asked where I was staying. I told him. I asked how long What's to Eat? had been in business.

"Five years next winter."

"Are you the sole proprietor?"

"Yes, I am. Well, better get back to the salt mine. Enjoying San Francisco?"

"Very much. Any suggestions for this inveterate tourist?"

"I suppose you've done all the usual stuff. Ever walked the Golden Gate?"

"Walked it? The bridge, you mean?"

"Yeah. Great views of the city on a nice day. Give it a try."

"I just might. I have a free day tomorrow. What's the weather forecast?"

"Same as always. Anything possible. Well, Mrs. Fletcher, thanks for calling on us. I'll look forward to reading one of your books someday."

"That would be nice, Mr. Frederickson."

The waitress who'd served me came running through the front door to where we stood. She carried what appeared to me to be a doggie bag. At least it looked like one. It had a dog's face on it. A long pink dog's tongue secured the top.

"For you," she said breathlessly.

"I'm afraid you've brought this to the wrong person. I'm embarrassed to say I didn't leave a crumb on my plate."

"Compliments of Mr. Frederickson," she said.

"Really?" I glanced at Frederickson, peeled the pink tongue from the bag and peered inside at something bulky wrapped in bubble–gum pink paper. I opened that up, too. It contained an enormous sandwich, and a large purple dinosaur cookie stuffed with gobs of whipped cream.

"Something to remember What's to Eat? by," he said.

"Oh, I don't think I need this to remember What's to Eat?" I said. "Believe me, Mr. Frederickson, I won't forget you."

A few hours later, the young man called "Petey" swung by the hotel with the prints. I came to the lobby and signed one: "To Robert Frederickson. Jessica Fletcher." Ordinarily, I would have said something cordial, like "Best Wishes," or, "All the Best." I wasn't in the mood.

Chapter Six

I returned to the suite and followed through on a decision I'd made to place a call to the home of Nancy Antonio, Ellie Steffer's godmother, in the hope of speaking with the teenage girl. It was answered on the first ring.

"Hello. May I please speak to Nancy Antonio?"

"Speaking."

"I was actually calling in the hope of speaking with Ellie."

"Ellie? Do I know you?"

"No. We haven't met. My name is Jessica Fletcher."

"What is your name?"

"Fletcher. Jessica Fletcher."

"And you wish to speak with Ellie."

"That's right."

"Concerning what?"

"A—personal matter."

"You're aware that Ellie is a child?"

"Yes."

"You say we haven't met. How did you get my

number? And what is this 'personal matter' you want to talk to her about?"

I decided honesty was the only policy to follow at this point. "I was given your name by Kimberly Steffer, and got your number from Information," I said.

"You've got to be kidding," she shouted, causing me to distance the receiver from my ear. Then she guffawed. "Let me get this straight. Kimberly told you to phone here and ask for Ellie? Is this some sort of joke? Who the hell are you anyway?"

"I'm a writer, Ms. Antonio. I was visiting—"

"The murder mystery writer?"

"Correct. I recently visited the Women's Correctional Facility to speak to some inmates there about writing. I met Kimberly Steffer under that circumstance."

"Well, now, that's just terrific," she said, sarcasm scorching the phone line. "What is Kimberly about to do, Mrs. Fletcher? Sell her story for a million bucks? Collaborate with you? What a great idea. But I assume you know that Kimberly is in prison because she committed a horrible crime. Murder! She murdered her husband. Is that the sort of person you like to collaborate with?"

"I'm not collaborating with—"

"Who do you think you are, Mrs. Fletcher? How dare you call here and bother Ellie for your own monetary gain? The poor girl has been through enough. I suggest you leave her—*us*—alone, or I'll call my attorney. Good-bye!"

I gently replaced the receiver in its base. She was

right, of course. Who did I think I was calling this youngster whom I didn't even know, and whose father had been brutally murdered? To top it off, I'd called on the suggestion of her stepmother, who'd been convicted of taking her father from her through the unspeakable act of murder.

I spent the next few minutes in my suite at the St. Francis considering what had transpired that day—my brief meeting at the Women's Correctional Facility with Kimberly Steffer at which I pledged my best efforts to exonerate her of the murder of her husband; my conversation at the *Chronicle* with Bobby McCormick, and his expression of belief in Kimberly's innocence; lunch at What's to Eat?, and subsequent exchange with Mark Steffer's former partner in the restaurant, Robert Frederickson, whom I labeled in my own mind as smarmy; and now my awkward, ill-advised call to Nancy Antonio in the hope of speaking with Kimberly's stepdaughter, Ellie.

I had to admit to myself that I hadn't made much headway. Not that I expected my initial efforts to shed sudden bright light on things. But I had hoped to learn something, anything that would, if nothing else, give me—as well as Kimberly Steffer—a reason for optimism.

I sat back in my chair and expelled a sustained breath. Kimberly's journal was on a table next to me. I picked it up and began reading again. The fact that I dozed off says nothing about my interest in the journal. It had been a long and stressful day.

I awoke with a start at five. I heard the phone

ringing, but it sounded far away. Very far away. In another state. Another world.

I stood groggily and tried to hone in on the location of the phone. Phones. The suite had more phones than my house back in Cabot Cove.

I realized one was on the table next to where I'd dozed off. "Hello?" I said, sounding drunk.

"Jessica?"

"Yes. George?"

"Yes" came through a familiar laugh. "I'm here. In San Francisco."

"You are? Of course you are. I was sleeping and—"

"Sorry to have awoken you."

"No, please. How wonderful to hear your voice. You're at the Mark?"

"Yes. Just checked in. I wondered if you were up to a welcoming drink. Presumptuous, of course, to suggest a formal welcome for me but—"

"I think it's a splendid idea."

"I'll head there straight away."

"I have a better idea, George. Give me a half hour and we'll meet at the Top of the Mark, right where you are. The views are splendid."

"I know those views well, Jessica. But they'll be twice as appealing with you at my side."

Trust George Sutherland to say the right thing, at the right time.

As I entered the sweeping, circular room that is the Top of the Mark, I scanned tables in search of

George. No sign of him. But I did see what I was certain were groups of law enforcement officers. Not that any of them were personally familiar to me. It's just that with rare exceptions, cops, at least American cops, are easy to spot in any room, in any hotel in the world. There's something about them, a self-assuredness that comes with the power they're capable of wielding, a set of the jaw, their choice in suits, and most of all a constant sense of their surroundings that civilians simply don't have. I should add that this easy recognition doesn't always hold true for the swelling numbers of female cops. Maybe that's why they've proved themselves to be especially effective when being nondescript is important.

The room was filling quickly, and I decided to grab a table. I'd been seated at one of the last remaining window tables, and a waitress had taken my order, when George made his entrance. He spotted me right away and threaded his way through knots of people with surprising grace for a big man. He stopped a few times to greet colleagues also attending the seminar, finally reached my table, and smiled broadly.

I stood. We shook hands. He kissed my cheek and said, "How do you do it, Jessica?"

"Do what?"

"Manage to look younger with each year."

"First of all, I don't. Second, I love hearing it."

He sat across the small table from me, casually crossed one leg over the other, and sighed. "It is very good to be here with you," he said. "Very good indeed."

"For me, too," I said.

We took a moment to scrutinize each other. No one would argue George's Scottish heritage. His cheekbones were prominent, his nose aquiline, his skin ruddy. A few extra strands of gray now blended at the temples with his brown hair tinged with red. He was dressed as he was the first time I met him for tea at Brown's Hotel in London; dark brown tweed jacket with leather patches at the elbows, a V-neck sweater the color of a fresh-baked biscuit, white shirt, brown tie, tan slacks, and ankle-high brown boots polished to a deep sheen. But what I remembered most—and that was still abundantly evident—was the kindness in his eyes, which were the color of Granny Smith apples. I've never tried to define "handsome," but George Sutherland would certainly do.

"Let's get the nitty-gritty out of the way," he said. "How long will you be in town?"

"Another week. I've already been here a week. My latest book has finally hit the bookstores, and I've fulfilled my obligatory book-signing appearances, not to mention television and radio appearances in New York, Boston, and Chicago. San Francisco marks the end of the tour. I've decided I deserve a vacation, so I'm tacking on an extra week here."

He asked our waitress what single-malt scotches were available, and chose a Knockando on the rocks.

"You've traveled a long way from Scotland to have a single malt scotch," I said.

"Can't afford to drink it at home," he said.

We toasted when his drink arrived, the rims of our glasses touching as gently as a kiss.

"All right, Jessica, you go first. You have six minutes to fill me in on the past year."

"I thought I did that in my last letter."

"You tried. But I think I know you better. Your life sounded—well, sounded as though it lacked its usual excitement."

"Hardly. But the sense of excitement quickly wanes after the rush of it is over." I brought him up to date on a few aspects of my recent life that hadn't made it into my letter. "Your turn," I said. "You have five minutes."

"You've stolen a minute from me."

"So that we can get through with the 'This Is Your Life' portion of the evening, and get on to more substantive things."

"All right." He was finished in two minutes. "Now, your turn to provide 'substance.' "

"Will murder do?"

"Fiction or fact?"

"Fact."

"Yes, I think that will do just fine. You're involved again."

"You make it sound nefarious on my part."

"Dangerous is more like it, Jessica. You do know I'm quite fond of you, and worry when you stray from your trusty typewriter and intrude on my turf."

"Your turf?"

"*Real* murder. My bailiwick. If you insist upon becoming involved in the real thing, I suggest you apply for a job with the Yard."

"I'd love it."

"Yes, I'm sure you would. Has this murder in which you're currently interested fallen into your lap, as they say? Or is it something you've pursued?"

"It fell into my lap. Or, more accurately, it fell into my briefcase."

"Did it? Sure you didn't instigate things? We have a saying in Scotland: *'He that blaws in the stoor fills his ain een.'* "

"Whoever said that Scots speak English was wrong. And what does that mean?"

"He that stirs up trouble, finds himself in it."

"Lesson received and understood. George, does the name Kimberly Steffer ring a bell?"

"Of course," he replied, not even blinking. "Pity what happened to her. She's the young writer—children's books, if I'm not mistaken—who murdered—allegedly—her husband. Name, Mark. Owned a restaurant here in San Francisco. She was born and raised in England but moved here when she married the chap. Our infamous British tabloids loved that case. Practically got as much coverage as Fergie and Di."

I nodded in appreciation of his powers of recall.

"Why do you ask?" he said.

"A complicated story, George, which should come as no surprise considering I've ended up involved—

to a degree. A couple of days ago I visited a women's prison outside San Francisco. My publicity agent arranged for me to speak to the inmates about writing. I emphasized journal writing.

"When I got back to town, I was surprised to discover that one of the inmates had planted a large black book in my bag. It turned out to be a diary. A diary filled with accounts of a trial, and proclaiming the author's innocence."

"And the author was Kimberly Steffer."

"Exactly."

"Go on," he instructed.

"I read the diary and was mesmerized. So I went back to the prison and met with Ms. Steffer. We spoke briefly in the Visitor's Room, and she divulged some interesting facts to me."

"Such as?"

"She mentioned a partner in her husband's restaurant as being capable of the murder. And she mentioned a stepdaughter, who she believes knows who *really* killed her husband."

"I can see why your interest has been piqued."

"I'm not convinced she murdered her husband," I said.

"Nor am I."

"You aren't?"

"No. Kimberly comes from a lovely, close family. Some members of that family paid me a visit at Scotland Yard when Kimberly was charged with her husband's murder. I listened to their pleas, of course, and was sufficiently impressed to personally look into the case. There wasn't much I could do. San Francisco is hardly my jurisdiction. But I did try to gather what information was available to me. I called Ms. Steffer's defense attorney here, even got hold of the prosecutor in the case. The case against her was purely circumstantial. No eyewitnesses. No smoking gun or bloody dagger. A combination of a zealous and skilled prosecuting attorney pitted against what, in my judgment from afar, was a somewhat inept defense attorney."

"Did her family give you any tangible information that might help establish her innocence?" I asked.

He shook his head. Then he leaned closer over the table, not so much because he didn't want to be overheard, but to emphasize the importance of what he was about to say. "Nothing tangible, Jessica. But I believed her family. Hardly what a veteran, hard-boiled officer of the law should be doing, but I did. Believed them, that is. I vividly remember looking into her father's eyes and *knowing* that everything he said about his 'little girl' was true. That she was, indeed, a genteel writer of children's books, incapable of killing anyone. Her father also convinced me of his daughter's love for this man, Mark, whom she'd married. I found it as inconceivable as did he that his daughter had murdered him."

"Sheer instinct on your part," I said.

"Yes."

"I've never considered you to be hard-boiled."

"I have my moments. There was some especially

gripping testimony from a cabdriver, as I remember, and accounts from several other witnesses."

"Some with axes to grind," I offered. "At least according to Kimberly."

"I heard that, too. Scuttlebutt from American colleagues. I received a touching thank-you note from her family for my efforts. It made me want to do something more than make a few phone calls. But my hands were tied. Have you run across the illustrator for her books?"

"Illustrator? No. You obviously know a lot more about the case than I do. I just got started."

"I can't remember the bloke's name. He'd had a legal problem with Ms. Steffer sometime before her husband's murder. It seems he sued her in court here in The States."

"Sued her for what?"

"It came down to, I believe, his claim that she owed him money. I have no idea what the amount was, but it did revolve around a contract that existed between them. Coming back to me now. He alleged that his percentage in their contractual arrangement should have been considerably higher because the books went on to become international best-sellers. He didn't prevail in that suit. After all, a written agreement is just that. He returned to London after his defeat in your courts."

"Was he questioned about the murder?"

"I don't know about here, but I contacted him. Ms. Steffer's family raised his name with me. He didn't want to meet with me, nor was he obligated to. We had a brief chat on the phone. I always remember his final comment. He said, 'As far as I'm concerned, Kimberly got what she deserved.' Or something equally poetic."

I shook my head. "I'm confused, George. Why would *he* murder Mark Steffer?"

He finished his scotch, said with a shrug, "He wouldn't be the first person to kill someone close to a hated rival. I asked whether you'd run across him because after staying in London for a short time—he's British—he returned to The States to live. Out here on the West Coast."

He looked at his watch. "Good heavens, Jessica, I'm afraid I must run out on you. Tonight is the opening dinner. I still haven't unpacked, and have business to tend to before the 'festivities' begin."

"I understand, George."

"Tell you what," he said, "this series of seminars will keep me busy for the next couple of days. But I've made a hard-boiled decision as we've been talking."

"Oh?"

"I've decided that I deserve a holiday, too. I intend to call my travel agent the moment I get to my room and book a later flight. A week later."

My pleasure was obviously written all over my face.

"I'd like nothing more than to spend a week in this splendid city with an equally splendid woman named Jessica Fletcher."

"Sure you can?" I asked.

"A chief inspector can do anything, Jessica."

I smiled. "Run along," I said. "I don't feel nearly as deprived losing you tonight, knowing I'll have an entire week in your company."

"Care to attend some of the seminars?" he asked. "Might be instructive."

"Thanks for the offer, George, but I think not. I don't want to develop a reputation for hanging around with the wrong crowd."

"A wise decision."

"Know what I think I might do tomorrow?"

"No, what?" He looked for our waitress and reached for his wallet.

"My treat, George."

"So you've become a woman of the 'nineties, Jessica."

"If buying you a drink labels me that, feel free to pay."

"Remember, *'Fair maidens wear nae purses.'*"

"Another Scottish expression?"

"Yes. We Scots may have a reputation for being tight with money, but we balk at having women pay when in mixed company."

We both laughed.

"Tomorrow," he said. "You were about to tell me what you might do."

"Oh. Right. Have you ever walked across the Golden Gate Bridge?"

"No."

"Want to? If you do, I'll postpone it until you're free."

"Better do it while the urge is strong, Jessica. That's what you have on tap tomorrow?"

"Weather permitting."

"Well, whatever you do, do it carefully. Wear heavy shoes."

"Why?"

"To give you ballast in a strong wind."

We both stood. He kissed me on the cheek. Our eyes lingered on each other as we promised to keep in close touch at our respective hotels. And he was gone, swallowed by the large crowd waiting at the captain's desk for tables to open up.

Chapter Seven

Once George disappeared through the crowd, and buoyed by the thought of having him around for a whole week, I left the Top of the Mark to head out for some evening sight-seeing.

Fisherman's Wharf: I snacked on a crab cocktail from a sidewalk vendor, purchased a lovely tooled leather address book from a local artisan, and enjoyed a cup of Irish coffee at a communal table in the Buena Vista Café, where that scrumptious concoction was first introduced to this country by famed San Francisco columnist Stan Delaplane. From there, I hailed a taxi and asked the driver to take me down Lombard Street, "the world's crookedest street," which he did, and which I found to be fun even though I'd done it numerous times before.

My internal dinner bell went off, and I headed for Chinatown, *the* Chinatown, for an appetizer of minced squab wrapped in lettuce leaves, and lobster broiled in ginger sauce, at Celadon.

I arrived back at the Westin St. Francis at eleven

feeling wonderful. I thought of Abraham Maslow, the pioneering psychologist, who identified one of the signs of sanity as having the ability to recognize and enjoy "peak experiences"—those moments, large or small, when you are at one with the world, and when your senses explode in celebration. A lovely climbing rosebush wet with dew; a sudden snap of cool air after a period of hot and humid weather; a baby's smile; a lick from a loving dog's warm, wet tongue.

The physical beauty of San Francisco. Excellent food. Bracing air. Friendly people. The anticipation of a week with Chief Inspector George Sutherland.

At that moment, according to Maslow, my sanity was beyond debate.

"Good morning, Mrs. Fletcher. It's seven o'clock, and sixty-one sunny degrees outside. Have a wonderful day."

"I certainly intend to," I said to the recorded wake-up message.

I'd decided to skip the gym that morning, and to ease into the day at a more leisurely pace. I'd done plenty of walking the night before. Besides, having decided to take a stroll across the Golden Gate Bridge would make up for any lost time on the exercise bike.

It had never occurred to me to take such a walk. But Robert Frederickson had suggested it. And the cabdriver who'd driven me down the hairpin turns of Lombard Street last night had casually mentioned that crossing the Golden Gate on foot was one of his favorite things to do on a day off.

And so I decided it offered a chance to do something different in a city rife with different things to do.

I wanted an early start; new adventures are always more enjoyable, at least to this early riser, when experienced in cool, crisp morning air. The vision of the bridge showered in the early morning light was palpably pleasant.

I turned on a small television set in the bathroom, adjusted the water in the shower, got in, shampooed with a lovely almond shampoo provided by the hotel, and was in the act of vigorously washing my hair when I heard the phone ring. Although there was a phone in the bathroom, it was on the opposite wall. I hate decisions like that. Do I step out of the shower and drip water all over the floor? Try to towel off in time to catch who was calling? Ignore it, and let voice mail take a message?

I opted for the latter course of action. I knew that callers would be asked by a live operator whether they wished to leave a message with her, or to record it on my Voice Mail. Either way, I'd get it once I was out of the shower—provided the caller wanted me to receive a message. I thought as I dried off with one of the oversize, plush velvet towels how convenient it would be to have a waterproof telephone in the shower.

I peeked into my bedroom and saw the flashing

message light on that room's phone. Wrapped in my towel, I punched in numbers to activate Voice Mail.

"Good morning to you, lovely lady. George here. You've evidently gotten off to an early running start to the day, one of many admirable traits I've observed in you. Unless, of course, you're still sleeping, in which case I take back my compliment and will ring off in order not to disturb your much-needed slumber." He paused to see whether I'd pick up. When I didn't, he continued: "Jessica, the reason I'm calling is to give you the name of the gentleman I'd mentioned last night over drinks. You know, the illustrator for Kimberly Steffer's books. His name is Brett Pearl." He spelled it for me. "I looked the chap up in the phone book, and he's listed as living in Sausalito, with an office in downtown San Francisco. Evidently doing quite well, wouldn't you say? Have a good day, as you Americans are fond of saying, and be in touch. Bye for now."

I slipped into the terry cloth robe bearing the St. Francis insignia, went to the desk in the living room, and found the white pages. I looked under Pearl. *Pearl, Brett, 508 Birch, Saus.*

Was it fate? I planned to cross the bridge from San Francisco to the Sausalito side. I wasn't sure whether I'd do a round-trip walk, or take the ferry back to the city. A few hours in the quaint village of Sausalito would give me time to recover and to make that decision. And, of course, to drop in unannounced on Mr. Brett Pearl: "Hi, I was in the neighborhood and thought—"

But by the time I was dressed and ready to venture out, I thought better of that plan. Walk across the bridge, Jess, but don't walk into trouble. What was that Scottish expression George Sutherland was fond of using? *"Better mak your feet your friends."* Translation: "Run for your life."

The taxi drove away, leaving me standing in awe at the San Francisco side of the almost two-mile-long, breathtaking red suspension bridge known worldwide as the Golden Gate. If it hadn't been modern, it would certainly qualify as the eighth wonder of the world. The fact that it was created by man—its chief engineer was a gentleman named Joseph Strauss, who oversaw the four-and-one-half-year construction project that culminated in 1937 with the punch of a telegraph key three thousand miles away in Washington, D.C., by President Roosevelt. That resulted in horns and whistles, and the biggest peacetime concentration of naval war vessels in history.

I'd read that the bridge was 260 feet high at midpoint in order to allow the navy's largest battleships to pass beneath it. I'd also read in my handy guidebook that on opening day, and before vehicles were allowed on it, more than 200,000 pedestrians swamped the bridge, their weight causing the center to drop as much as ten feet. Not to worry; it was designed to survive winds in excess of one hundred miles an hour, and to sway as much as twenty-seven feet at its center.

It wasn't perfect bridge-walking weather. What had started as a sunny, calm day had quickly deteriorated into an overcast, windy one, at least where I stood. I'd dressed for it. You learn to anticipate weather turns in Maine. I wore an ivory cable-knit sweater, sweatpants, sneakers, and my red, white, and blue windbreaker.

But I wasn't the only person to be undaunted by the wind and gray skies. Dozens of men, women, and children were on the bridge, some just completing their journeys, others starting out in the direction of Sausalito. I silently hoped they were all there to *walk* the bridge, and not to jump. In some quarters, the Golden Gate Bridge is as famous for those who don't make the return trip, as it is for its beauty.

I looked across the length of the span. Silly, I thought, to feel so much trepidation. Hundreds of people did it every day. I'm not exactly fond of heights, but I don't have any special aversion to them.

As I started out, I soon decided that the biggest threat to my safety were the automobiles whizzing by. The pedestrian walkway wasn't very wide; the cars seemed to be too close for comfort.

I continued. The farther I went, the more spectacular the view became. Although it remained misty on the bridge, shafts of sun seemed to explode from the gray clouds above, spotlighting the city's white and pastel buildings, and newer curtain-wall skyscrapers. Another shaft played on the millions of ripples in San Francisco Bay. It was spectacular; my gasp was involuntary.

I forged ahead, the wind stinging my face, the slight sway of the bridge beneath my feet actually pleasant, like being on a mighty ocean liner. The bay was dotted with sailboats and a few brave windsurfers.

Others on the bridge were in a good mood. Almost everyone smiled as they passed and said something in greeting, which I returned. I felt marvelous. My blood raced as I picked up my pace. How far had I come? I'd estimated it would take about an hour to complete the journey to Vista Point on the Marin County side. I'd been walking for a half hour. That should put me at mid-span. Judging from the cluster of people there, that was exactly the point I'd reached. Dozens of cameras were pointed in every direction.

Despite the number of fellow-tourists, I felt pleasantly alone. I could feel my heart beating in my chest, and I wiped at tears caused by the wind. As I drew deep breaths, I felt giddy. Did I look foolish? Childish? No matter. Times in our lives when we get to feel like children again are too precious to let pass.

I slowly turned to take in 360 degrees of my surroundings. To my left were the hills of Sausalito and Marin County. With my back to the bridge railing, I could see over the traffic the vast expanse of the Pacific Ocean. Another 90-degree turn and I looked back to the direction from which I'd come. And then I returned to my original position, peering out over San Francisco Bay and across to the City by the Bay. It was like an Impressionist painting. Pissarro? Monet? Degas? Perhaps Renoir.

What happened next was hardly impressionistic. It was more out of the school of *"Art Brute"*—brutal realism.

It started when an especially strong gust of wind caused me to throw back my head and to laugh. I closed my eyes for a second. And then I felt the strength of a hand, connected to a strong arm, grasp the back of my neck and shove me forward. Simultaneously, another hand—presumably belonging to the same person—grabbed the bottom of my windbreaker and attempted to pick me up and over the railing.

I fought to maintain a hold. I shouted, but my voice was carried out to sea by the wind, inaudible to even me. I tried to twist in order to see who was trying to push me to my death, but failed.

And then, as suddenly and unexpectedly as this unknown person had come up behind me, he, or she, was gone. I was draped over the railing when the pressure ceased, gasping for breath, shaking uncontrollably. Finally—it seemed minutes, although it was only seconds—I stood and turned, my knees trembling to the extent I wasn't certain they would support me. It had happened so fast that no one, it seemed, had seen the attack. They were too busy marveling at the views, and taking pictures of them.

Except for a young girl, perhaps ten, who said, "Are you okay, lady?"

"Yes. No. I mean—" I looked past her in search of the person who'd tried to kill me. Whoever it was had disappeared into the crowds walking the bridge that morning.

"Did you see who tried to push me over?" I asked her.

"Push you? No, ma'am. You look like you're sick, that's all."

"Sick? No. I'm fine. Thank you for asking."

I knew that if I didn't start walking again, the sudden nausea I was experiencing would worsen. I ruled out continuing to the Sausalito side of the bridge. I wanted to be back in San Francisco, in my suite, safe and secure. I also wanted to report the incident to the police.

Oddly, even though I was in a hurry, I started off walking slower than before in what might have appeared to be slow-motion determination, a drunk making sure each step connects with the ground.

But my need to get off the bridge took over, and I actually began to jog. Me, who has never jogged in her life. And finally, I broke out into a run, as if my life depended on it—which I was fairly certain it did.

I reached the San Francisco side in what might have been the fastest mile ever recorded by a female mystery writer from Maine who was on the wrong side of fifty.

Chapter Eight

"I was walking across the Golden Gate Bridge. I'd reached midway and had stopped to admire the scenery. Suddenly, someone, a man or a woman, grabbed me and tried to push me off. It happened so quickly that I really can't provide you with any more details. I'm sorry."

San Francisco Detective Walter Josephs looked as though he might be nearing retirement. His graying black hair was the consistency of steel wool, and was as tousled as mine, although he hadn't had to cross a bridge to achieve it. There was a pretty good supply of stubble on his face that was not the result of attempting to grow a beard. More a matter of being in a hurry to get to work and deciding to skip the razor. He appeared to be tired, which might have been the reason he seldom looked at me as I recounted for him my frightening experience on the Golden Gate that morning.

He stopped writing on a pad, rubbed his eyes, glanced at me, and said, "Okay, Mrs. Fletcher, you say someone tried to push you off the bridge. Go over it again with me, only try to be more specific this time around." He wasn't being nasty. He just had that flat way of saying things that cops develop over too many years of taking statements.

I told my story again, adding, "I wish I could be more specific, Detective Josephs. But the fact is, I simply did not have an opportunity to see the person who did it. I was too shaken. By the time I turned around he, or she, was gone. There were many people on the bridge today."

"Usually are," he muttered. "You don't even know if it was a man or woman?"

"No."

"You said whoever it was was pretty strong. Probably a man, huh?"

"A fair assumption, I suppose, but not necessarily an accurate one."

He placed his pen on the pad and smiled for the first time. "I have to admit, Mrs. Fletcher, that I wondered whether you really were *the* Jessica Fletcher."

I returned his smile. "I assure you I am."

"Yeah. I know you are. You're right. You are the mystery writer."

"Yes, for better or for worse."

"The reason I'm sure you are is that I read the article about you in the *Chronicle*. You look a little different than the picture they ran of you. No offense."

"None taken."

"What I'm thinking is that I can't imagine why

somebody would try to push you off the Golden Gate. I mean, if somebody wanted to kill you, there's easier ways to do it. Shoot you. Run you over. Poison in your crabmeat. But you know all about that, killing off people in your books."

"Somehow," I said, "it sounds a lot more ominous when you're talking about *me*."

"I suppose it would." He sat back and crossed his arms. "Know of any enemies here in San Francisco?" he asked.

"No," I replied. "Except that—"

He uncrossed his arms and leaned forward, his eyes wider now as he awaited my explanation. "Except what, Mrs. Fletcher?"

"Well, I wouldn't swear that I've made enemies since coming here a week ago, but I have rubbed a few people the wrong way."

"Have you? How?"

"I've been—I've been looking into a murder case that took place in this city a couple of years ago. The Kimberly Steffer case."

"I know it well. Why?"

"Why am I looking into it?"

He nodded. "Basis for the plot of your next novel?"

"Hardly. That's not the way I go about plotting my murders. I only write fiction. Not true crime."

"Okay. So my question demonstrates a certain ignorance on my part about how murder mystery books get plotted. Why are you interested in the Steffer case?"

"I met Kimberly in prison last week. I went there to talk to the inmates about writing. She was in the audience."

"Hmmmm," he said. "How's she doing?"

"As well as anyone can be expected under the circumstances. Not a very pleasant place."

"Not supposed to be. So, Mrs. Fletcher, you still haven't told me why you've decided to look into her case."

"Some people think she's innocent," I said.

"Including you?"

"Yes. I think so."

"Include me," he said without emotion or inflection.

"You?"

"Yup."

"Did you investigate that homicide?"

"No. I've been on desk duty ever since some whack job high on something decided to shoot me in the back. Lucky I can walk."

"How dreadful."

"Yeah. He walked on a technicality. But no, Mrs. Fletcher, I wasn't involved in the investigation into Mark Steffer's murder. But I followed it close. Like most people, only I had a little more inside info."

"I would imagine."

"Between you and me, the investigation was not destined to win any awards for police work. A classic case of deciding who did it, and using what you come up with to 'prove' it. Like I said, that's between us."

"I understand."

"She never should have been convicted. Not on what we turned up. Her lawyer was a joke. She had plenty of money but went for flash over substance. The jury must have been out to lunch."

"Wasn't there an appeal?"

"Sure. But the original judge had been okay. No errors. Just a lot of sighs at her attorney's posturing. The verdict stood on appeal."

"Not our system of jurisprudence's finest hour."

"I've seen worse, like in my case. Anyway, Mrs. Fletcher, you said in poking your nose into the Steffer case you might have made an enemy or two. Correction. I didn't mean anything negative by putting it that way."

"I didn't take it negatively," I said. " 'Poking my nose into it' is an apt way of describing it. And yes, I might have rubbed someone the wrong way."

"Who?"

I shrugged. "No one who knew I intended to take my stroll on the Golden Gate this morning."

"Who *did* know?"

"No one."

"Not possible."

"It's not?"

"No. How did you get to the bridge?"

"Cab."

"Get the driver's name?"

"No."

"Where are you staying?"

"The Westin St. Francis."

"Nice hotel."

"The best."

"Nobody there knew you were planning your walk?"

"I don't think so. Oh, I may have mentioned it to my waitress at breakfast this morning."

"Uh-huh. Continue."

"I think I told the doorman. I had to wait with him until he hailed a taxi for me. You aren't suggesting that—?"

"Who else?"

"Let me see. The cabdriver who drove me last night. It was his suggestion that prompted me to do it."

"Name?"

"No idea. Actually, he was the second person to suggest the walk."

"Who was the first?"

"Robert Frederickson. He—"

"Mark Steffer's former partner in that cutesy kids restaurant."

"Exactly."

"You get around, Mrs. Fletcher."

"I try."

"Frederickson suggested you take that walk?"

"Yes."

"What do you think of Mr. Frederickson?"

"Handsome. A little too slick for my taste."

He laughed. "Oily guy."

"Yes."

"Who else knew you'd be out on the bridge today?"

"No one. Oh, I mentioned the possibility to an old friend."

"Who happens to be?"

"Chief Inspector George Sutherland of Scotland Yard."

"George? He's a friend?"

"Yes. You obviously know him."

"Sure. Hell of a guy. Worked his side of a murder case with me years back. He's here in San Fran at the FBI seminar?"

"Yes."

"Give the crusty old Scot my best."

"In those words?"

"Sure. That's it for the list?"

"I think so. No. I mentioned it to my publicity agent this morning when she called."

"What is your publicity agent's name?"

"Camille. Camille Inken. Surely you don't think that—"

He smiled and put the cap on his pen. "See, Mrs. Fletcher? You tell one person something, you tell half a dozen. And they tell another half dozen. Pretty soon, the entire population of San Francisco knows."

"Point well taken."

He stood and I followed his cue. "Feel safe enough to go back to the St. Francis? Like a lift?"

"No, I'm fine. But thank you for the offer."

"I insist."

"Then, I guess I accept. Can't say no to a detective when he insists."

He pulled a large manila envelope from a desk drawer and motioned for me to follow him. We climbed into his unmarked car parked in front of police headquarters, and minutes later were in front of the hotel. "Buy you a drink, Mrs. Fletcher?" he asked. "I'm off duty."

"At this hour of the morning?"

"Middle of the night for me. I've been on since midnight."

"I'm afraid a drink is the last thing I need, Detective Josephs. But thank you anyway."

"Mind if I ask you a favor?"

"Ask and I'll see if I mind," I said.

He hesitated before saying, "Believe it or not, Mrs. Fletcher, I'm writing a cop novel. I'm about halfway through. I'd really appreciate it if you'd take a look at it." He smiled his most ingratiating smile, picked up the manila envelope from where he'd placed it between us, and handed it to me.

I took it and said, "I'd be delighted and flattered to read it, Detective. And I'm sure you'd be willing to do a favor for me in return."

"Tell me what it is and I'll decide."

"What's fair is fair," I said. "I'd like to see the files on the Steffer case." I mirrored his smile.

He smacked his lips and took a deep breath. "You drive a hard bargain for a writer, Mrs. Fletcher."

"Not such a hard bargain," I said. "I'm not asking to take any files with me. I'd just like to *peek* at them. In your presence." When he continued to ponder what I'd suggested, I added, "My publisher has published a number of very good books written by former law enforcement officers like yourself. If I think your manuscript has merit—"

"Okay," he said. "It's a deal. But you're not to breathe a word of this. Understood, Mrs. Fletcher?"

"Understood."

"It's strictly unofficial. On my off hours."

"Of course."

"When do you want to see the files?"

"How about now? You said you were off duty."

"Okay. When will you read my manuscript?"

"Tonight."

"Let's go."

When we were back in his office, he told me to sit tight. He returned quickly. "Okay, Mrs. Fletcher, here's the Steffer files." He handed me a disk. "You can access them on my computer here in the office, but you can't leave with it. Understood?"

"Loud and clear," I said.

His computer was on. He inserted the disk and pulled up the files. "You sit here, Mrs. Fletcher. I've got something else to do. Anybody comes in, tell 'em you're doing part-time work for me."

"Okay."

"And remember, Mrs. Fletcher, this is between you and me."

"Yes, sir!"

He left, and I scanned the first file:

Phillipe Fernandez, driver with the Express Cab Service, claims to have driven Kimberly Steffer from the mall where Mark Steffer's restaurant is located, to the Embarcadero Center. Fernandez gave a positive ID of Steffer. Said he picked her up at 3:15 P.M.

As I wrote Fernandez's name on a piece of paper, the door opened. It was Detective Josephs. "Find something interesting," he asked, positioning himself to view the computer screen, and the paper on which I'd written the name. "Phillipe," he said. "That's the cabbie." He rolled his eyes. "A monument to credibility. His glasses looked like aviator goggles."

"Yes, I've heard that," I said, remembering Bobby McCormick's description of the taxi driver's eyeglasses.

"Even the judge laughed when the defense demonstrated his less than twenty-twenty vision. But the jury didn't seem to care. Well, Mrs. Fletcher, I'm glad to see I could be of some help. I'll be here all day tomorrow if you want to call and let me know how much you enjoyed my manuscript."

"This is all I get to see of the Steffer files?" I said.

"Afraid so. Look, maybe we can—"

A man poked his head into Josephs' office. "Walter, you on?"

"No. I was just leaving."

"Sorry, babe, but you're here, you catch it. We've got a jumper on Golden Gate."

Detective Josephs looked at me and frowned.

"A jumper?" I asked. "Someone has jumped off the bridge?"

"Who's she?" the other detective asked about me.

"A—friend. All right. Let's go." To me: "Sorry, Mrs. Fletcher. Call me tomorrow. Maybe we can work something out."

"I certainly will call you tomorrow," I said, standing and getting ready to leave.

"And hey, Mrs. Fletcher, be sure to read Chapter Four. Fry your hair. Have a nice day."

Chapter Nine

"Police have ruled the plunge of a man early this morning from the Golden Gate Bridge an apparent suicide. It is the twenty-third suicide from the bridge this year. The victim's identification is still being withheld, pending notification of family." And now, turning to sports, here's . . ."

I turned off the TV in my suite and shook my head. That was it? That was the extent of the play the media planned to give the story of a person leaping to his death from the world's most famous bridge?

I had to remind myself, of course, that jumping from the Golden Gate was not an especially unique or startling event in San Francisco, any more than a mugging was in New York City. Twenty-third suicide of the year? Back home in Cabot Cove, *one* suicide was big news, worthy of weeks of breakfast gossip at Mara's Dockside Luncheonette.

I then found myself wondering how the San Francisco police made a determination of suicide when someone fell to his death from the Golden Gate. Failing an eyewitness, how could anyone be certain that a victim hadn't been pushed over the edge? Hadn't been murdered?

Someone had certainly tried to kill me that morning by "helping" me over the railing. And although there had been many other people within viewing distance of the event, no one seemed to have seen it happen. If my attacker had succeeded, I, too, would have been considered a suicide, although probably generating more media coverage because I was from out-of-town, and had achieved a modicum of fame through my books.

I'd left police headquarters ambivalent about what to do, or where to go next. I decided as I walked that I'd been denying the impact of the attempt upon my life just hours earlier. Once I made that admission to myself, it hit me like the proverbial ton of bricks, causing my legs to weaken, and my breathing to go shallow and rapid. I hailed a passing cab and told the driver to take me to my hotel. But I quickly changed my mind. I needed to eat, and to draw upon the splendid day it had become.

The driver dropped me at Fisherman's Wharf. I took a table in a pleasant outdoor café, sated my sudden appetite with a large crabmeat salad and two glasses of iced coffee, and renewed my energy by soaking up the spirit of passersby as they went about their day on the famous wharf.

I did some window-shopping back at Union Square before returning to my suite. The only purchase I made was a bouquet of fresh pink tulips from one of several flower markets on the square,

the vendors owing their existence to Michael de
Young who in the late 1800s allowed Italian, Bel-
gian, and Irish youngsters to sell their flowers in
front of his office building without police harass-
ment. They were eventually licensed in 1904, and
their colorful stands, along with the chess players,
soapbox orators (shades of London's Hyde Park Corner), panhandlers, and hand-holding lovers give the
square's famous park much of its character. I
promptly placed my purchase in a vase supplied by
room service. I often buy flowers for my hotel room
when traveling because even the most opulent hotel
benefits from personalizing.

I was disappointed that George hadn't called. I'd
left a message for him after leaving police headquarters. Must be in meetings all day.

I looked at my watch. The afternoon had slid by too
quickly. It was almost five o'clock. I was tired, could
easily have succumbed to fatigue and taken a nap.
But I didn't want to do that because I knew I'd wake
up groggy and lacking energy. George's conference
would be winding down for the day. Should I try to
call him again? I decided instead to head for the Mark
Hopkins, call him from the lobby, and take my
chances that he'd be free for the evening.

I really needed to talk to him about my misadven-
ture that morning. I'd thought about calling Mort
or Seth back home to discuss the incident, but
didn't want to worry them. In the past, when I'd
called from a distant city to report an attempt on my
life, or some other imbroglio in which I'd become

embroiled, they'd responded by jumping on a plane and racing to my side. Sort of the "damsel in distress" reaction. But I didn't want that. Despite their sterling intentions, they invariably complicated things for me. Bless them. But better they remain in Cabot Cove.

Discussing my incident on the bridge with Detective Josephs that morning hadn't done much to satisfy my need to share it with others. I glanced over at a table on which I'd put his manuscript. I'd promised to read it that night, which I would do, of course. But he wouldn't get any substantive response to it from me until he'd lived up to his part of the bargain. I needed more time with his computer files on the Mark Steffer murder case. You give a little, you get a little. You give a lot, you get a lot. That would be my operative ground rule from now on when dealing with the detective.

As I closed my door behind me, I heard the faint ringing of the phone inside the suite. Go back and answer? By the time I dug out my magnetic card, aka key, from my purse, it would probably be too late. Whoever was calling could leave a message. If it was George, I'd see him soon enough.

As I rode down in the elevator, I changed my mind about surprising George at the Mark Hopkins. Simply showing up would place an unfair pressure on him in the event he'd made other plans for the evening, personal or professional.

The lobby of the St. Francis was bustling that late afternoon. Well-dressed businesspeople mingled with less well-dressed tourists, many of whom had made the hotel's famous lobby part of their sightseeing itinerary. The St. Francis is considered by travel writers to be the grand belle of San Francisco hotels, with its stately marble columns, breathtaking oversize flower arrangements, and rococo gold balconies.

There was a pay phone on a wall next to a house phone that sat on a marble shelf. A woman was on the house phone. As I approached, she slammed down the receiver and spun around. The anger on her face mirrored what she'd done to the phone.

I stopped to wait for her to walk away. But she didn't. She remained there, mumbling to herself, her face twisted in rage, her hand still gripping the receiver.

I decided to avoid her and to look for another pay phone. As I headed for a long, sweeping hallway off the lobby, a loud female voice from behind stopped me in my tracks. *"Mrs. Fletcher!"*

I turned to see the same woman who'd vented her anger on the telephone walking toward me. Her eyes were open wide, her lips squeezed tightly together. Every vein in her neck had swelled. She was a big woman with a big bosom, and with a mop of brown, frizzy hair topping off her frame. Everything about her was large, including her vocal cords.

She growled my name again, punctuating it this time with a question mark. She stopped a few feet away, shifted her weight to one leg, and crossed her arms over her chest. We held our standoff until she again said my name. This time it was punctuated with a strong exclamation point.

She seemed to be summoning me to come to her, a school principal beckoning a naughty student. I spun around with the intention of getting away from her. She was either a crazed fan, or a woman who should have stopped using drugs years ago. Either way, the morning's bizarre attempt on my life had sharpened my instincts, to say nothing of my sense of self-preservation. I headed for the front desk.

"Mrs. Fletcher!"

I faced her again. She'd come up directly behind me; she was within strangling distance, and breathing hard, eyes screaming. Then, she said in a much lower voice that trembled, "I am Nancy Antonio. Ellie's godmother."

"Oh."

I looked around. A clerk at the desk had come to where I stood. "Can I help you, Mrs. Fletcher?" he asked.

"No. I— Look, Ms. Antonio, I want you to know that I am *truly* sorry for making that phone call."

"As well you should be." She spoke slowly, deliberately, every word enunciated.

She uncrossed her arms. "Is there something you want to say to me, Mrs. Fletcher, now that we're face-to-face?" She was calm now. Maybe she had mercury for blood.

"No," I said. "I should not have tried to call your goddaughter. It's just that—"

"That's right, Mrs. Fletcher. You should not have

tried to talk to my goddaughter. And if you ever try again, I'll make you wish you were never born."

With that threat hanging in the air, she turned away and walked heavily, but quickly, through the lobby and out the revolving door.

"Whew!" I said, resting my elbows on the front desk. The clerk asked, "Is everything all right, Mrs. Fletcher?"

"Yes, everything is fine. Thank you for asking. I was about to use the pay phone over there and—"

"No need to do that, Mrs. Fletcher. Use the hotel phone right here."

He reached for it, but I said, "Thank you, but that's not necessary." I wanted privacy when I reached George Sutherland. I was no longer cavalier about whether he had other plans for the evening. I wanted his plans to include me, and hoped I'd reach him before he'd made another commitment. His comforting manner, to say nothing of a calming drink, were very much on my agenda.

I retraced my steps in the direction of the pay phone next to the marble shelf with the intention of calling George. At first, I didn't notice the small black leather purse next to the house phone. When I did, my heart tripped. Had it been left by the large, combative woman I'd just encountered? I looked around. I hadn't seen anyone use that phone except for Nancy Antonio, although I'd been distracted by her and wasn't keeping tabs.

I approached the purse as though it might be hot. A ticking bomb. My initial thought was to bring it to the front desk for delivery to lost and found. But I suddenly had a vision of not making it to the desk, of Ellie's godmother realizing she'd left her purse behind and returning for it, seeing me with it in my hands, and physically attacking me.

I decided to leave it next to the phone where I'd found it. I wanted nothing more to do with this woman, or her goddaughter. I would continue to investigate Kimberly's innocence, but would keep Ellie and the formidable Ms. Antonio out of it. At least for the moment.

But as I started to walk away, my eye went to a small piece of paper peeking out from beneath the purse. I glanced left and right. Confident that I wasn't being observed, I slipped it out and read: *"She's staying at the Westin St. Francis. We've got to warn her off, make it clear that her snooping is not welcome."*

I looked across the lobby and saw Nancy Antonio return through the revolving doors and head my way. I crumpled the note in my hand and quickly stepped behind a column that shielded me from her view, but that allowed me to observe her. She picked up her purse. A quizzical expression crossed her face as her eyes scanned the marble shelf, and then the floor. I held my breath. Would she extend the area of her search for the slip of paper to where I stood?

I was able to breathe again a few seconds later when she walked away and left the hotel.

Chapter Ten

They say that everything in life is timing. That day, my timing had been at once splendid and at once dreadful.

On the dreadful side, I'd chosen a bad time to take a walk on the Golden Gate Bridge, and to be looking for a pay phone in the lobby of the St. Francis.

On the splendid side, my call to George Sutherland at the Mark Hopkins caught him for the few minutes he was in his room between seminar commitments. "Are you free this evening?" I asked.

"Yes and no, Jessica. I'm hosting a cocktail party in twenty minutes. It seems we have more cocktail parties than working sessions, but I suppose that should come as no surprise."

"And after that?" I asked. "Free for dinner?"

"With you? Of course. You sound upset."

"Do I? I'm trying not to. But yes, I am upset. I need to talk to you."

"I'll pick you up in two hours. I'd come sooner, but this angersome party has me—"

"I'm leaving the hotel, George. I'll meet you at yours. Upstairs. At the Top of the Mark."

"Right on, Jessica. I'll be there as soon as I've discharged my obligations."

Under ordinary circumstances, I would have been delighted to be given a table with an unobstructed view of the Golden Gate. But after what had happened to me that morning, I found the sight of it off-putting. No, eerie was more apt.

Again, my timing was good and bad. I arrived at the Top of the Mark at the optimum time for witnessing the arrival of the city's fabled fog, that long-running theatrical event that is as much a tourist attraction in San Francisco as the cable cars and Alcatraz. By the time I was seated, the fog had obscured half the bridge, and was heading in my direction, swallowing buildings as it relentlessly made its predictable path across the city. As symbolic as it was of my horrifying experience on the bridge that morning, it was also mesmerizing. I stared at it until it had gulped the Top of the Mark, and me. And then, just as the fog had rolled in, so did George. He made his way quickly to my table, apologized for being late, and took the second chair. I had a half-finished perfect Manhattan in front of me. "Wonderful to see you, George," I said. "Let's find the waitress."

"Not for me," he said. "I've had enough to drink at the party. Hungry?"

"Yes."

"Then, let's get ourselves some dinner, someplace quiet where you can tell me what's upset you today."

Once a year—never more than that—I have a craving for sushi. I'd only had it twice before. The first time was in Tokyo, the second in New York. It will never rank on my list of favorite foods. But, as I say, I have this annual craving. And this was the night. Maybe stress and fear release some chemical in our bodies that activates a special taste gland. Maybe not. All I know is that George, dear man that he is, agreed to indulge my special need that evening, and took me to what is considered one of San Francisco's finest sushi restaurants, Restaurant Isuzu, in Japantown.

"You're a real friend, and a trooper, to come here, George," I said as we were seated in a pretty small room at the rear of the restaurant.

"For you, Jessica, I will do anything. Even sushi. I rather like the place. Charming. Besides, it will broaden my horizons, but not my waistline. When you think about it, you don't see many fat Japanese men or women."

"Sumo wrestlers?" I offered.

"There's an exception to everything."

"Thanks for stealing time for me, George. I know you're terribly busy and—"

He held up his hand. "Enough of that," he said. "Now, tell me what has upset you this fine day."

"Someone tried to kill me this morning."

"I would say that warrants a bit of upset. Where did this happen?"

"On the Golden Gate Bridge. I took that walk on the bridge I told you I was considering. Lovely morning. Lots of people doing the same thing. I stopped at mid-span to take in the views, and—well, someone tried to push me over the edge."

"What a horrible experience. You obviously managed to fight off the *bleck*."

"The what?"

"The *bleck*. The scoundrel. Go on. Who was it?"

"I don't know. I never saw him. Or her. When I fought back, the person backed off and disappeared into the crowd. I suppose if I'd turned around immediately I might have seen—the *bleck*—but I was too shaken."

A petite, pretty Japanese girl handed us warm towels to cleanse our hands, placed menus in front of us, and asked for our drink order. "Nothing for me, thank you," I said. "Just some club soda." George ordered a Japanese beer.

"What did you do after it happened?" he asked.

"I came back into town and went to the police. A Detective Josephs interviewed me. He says he knows you."

"Josephs? Yes, I vaguely recall someone with that name. Was he helpful?"

"Yes. And no. He's writing a novel and gave it to me to read."

"How inappropriate."

"Not really. We struck a deal. I read his novel in

exchange for the opportunity to review the Kimberly Steffer files."

He sat back and slowly shook his head. "You amaze me, Jessica. Someone tries to kill you, yet you forge ahead trying to solve a murder that happened years ago, in order to save a woman you barely know."

"Just an old fubdub, I suppose."

"Fubdub?"

"My turn to be colloquial. From Maine. Fubdub. A compulsive person. At any rate, that's what I did."

"Is his novel any good?"

"I don't know because I haven't read it yet. That's on my agenda for later tonight. Maybe we'd better order."

We perused the menus. Everything sounded wonderful to me. I checked George's expression. He looked pleased. "Find something you like?" I asked.

"Yes. They have tempura. Fried food always gets my vote. You?"

"The Futomaki sushi sounds good to me. A little bit of everything, including octopus."

George's expression changed to displeasure. I suppose considering where he's from, sushi doesn't appear on many pub menus. British food, including in Scotland where I've never been able to muster the courage to try *haggis*, has suffered for too long as offering up bad food. That was years ago. Some of my finest meals have been in the British Isles, especially a wonderful little pub George took me to one day for its famed shepherd's pie. The owner swears he's actually converted die-hard vegetarians to meat lovers. I didn't argue with him after tasting it.

George ordered his tempura, and I chose the sushi. I bit my lip when he requested that his tempura be well-done. He noticed my discomfort and said, "I like my fried food to be burned, Jess. The way my mother always cooked it." Our waitress, who I'm certain didn't understand him anyway, smiled and bowed.

"Jessica, why didn't you ring me up immediately to tell me what happened?"

"I'm not sure. It wasn't that I intended to keep it from you. I just preferred to tell you in person."

We talked of other things during dinner. It was over tea, and orange slices garnished with cherries, that I mentioned my confrontation with Ellie Steffer's godmother in the lobby of the St. Francis.

"That settles it," he said.

"Settles what?"

"You're moving *tonight* to the Mark Hopkins. I'll arrange for a room on my floor. You mustn't be in a hotel alone, not with the enemies you seem to have developed here in San Francisco." He spoke with finality, as if what he'd said wasn't open to discussion, and finished his beer.

"George," I said, "I appreciate your concern. Believe me, the moment I feel I'm in jeopardy, I'll move. Right next door to you. In the meantime, I prefer to stay put. They've given me the most magnificent suite. The staff is bending over backward to make my stay comfortable. Unless there's some dramatic reason for leaving, I prefer to stay put."

"Almost being pushed off the Golden Gate doesn't qualify as a dramatic reason?"

"Enough so to keep me off the bridge. But my suite and the hotel are perfectly safe."

"Then, I'll move to *your* hotel."

"You can't do that. You have the conference to consider. No, we'll leave things just as they are. For the moment."

"You're a dour woman, Jessica Fletcher."

"Dour? I don't consider myself morose."

"You aren't. You're dour. A misconception about the Scottish language. Dour. Stubborn."

"That I can accept."

"Care for an after-dinner drink before I see you safely back to your hotel? Some silki perhaps?"

I smiled. "It's saki, George. Saki. Not silki. And no thank you. I've had quite enough to drink for one day."

We took a cab to the St. Francis, and he escorted me to my suite. The moment I opened the door, I knew something was amiss. Lights were on that I was certain I'd turned off. The TV was playing.

"Hello?" I called.

George's five senses were instantly on alert. "Stay here, Jess," he said. He slowly approached the living room. "Who's here?" he barked.

I came up behind him and saw a man slowly get up from a wing chair that faced the television set.

"Detective Josephs!"

" 'Evening, Mrs. Fletcher."

"How did you get in here?" George asked.

"I asked. The badge helped. How the hell are you, George?" Josephs came across the room, his hand extended.

"Do I know you?" George asked.

"Of course you do. Walt Josephs. San Fran P.D."

George shook his hand. "I think I remember," he said. "Some conference a few years back."

"Right on."

"I still would like to know how—no, *why* you're here, Detective Josephs," I said.

I picked up the ringing phone. "Mrs. Fletcher, Roy Kramer. Assistant manager."

"Yes Mr. Kramer?"

"About the detective in your suite. We tried to dissuade him from entering, but he seemed to have official police business. I've checked his credentials with police headquarters, and they're in order. He said he could get a warrant if I insisted. I just felt that it was more prudent to—"

"No need to explain, Mr. Kramer. I would have done the same thing. But thank you for your concern."

When I hung up, Josephs said, "I found out something today I thought you'd be interested in knowing, Mrs. Fletcher."

"Such as?"

"I hope you don't think I'm pushy or anything, but I helped myself to a drink from your bar. I'm off duty. Happy to pay for it. Can I get you something, George?"

"I suggest you tell Mrs. Fletcher what it is you've come here to tell her, and then leave, Detective. She's had a long day and is quite fatigued."

"Oh, yeah, I know that. I hope you're not too tired to read my book, though."

"We can discuss that later," I said.

We all took seats before Josephs, remnants of his drink in his hand, said, "Remember that guy you mentioned to me? Brett Pearl?"

"The illustrator who worked on the books with Kimberly Steffer. Yes, I remember."

"And you know about the guy who went off the bridge today."

"I was in your office when you received the call."

"Seems they're one in the same."

"Oh, my. You're sure?"

"Yeah. His father confirmed the identity down at the morgue."

"A suicide?" George asked.

A shrug from Josephs. "The verdict's out on that."

"Meaning there's the possibility this Mr. Pearl was pushed off the bridge."

"Right on, George. A good possibility. We had a witness call this afternoon. Wouldn't identify herself, but she said she saw a struggle on the bridge about the time Pearl must have gone over."

"An anonymous witness?" George said.

"Just one witness?" I asked.

"So far. Like in your case, Mrs. Fletcher, having

lots of people around doesn't mean anybody sees anything—or wants to talk about it."

"Brett Pearl's death occurred shortly after the attempt on my life. Do you think it might have been the same person who tried to kill me?"

Another shrug. "Could be. But I'll tell you this. If that's the case, you're one strong lady. Not to mention lucky."

"How I successfully defended myself is an enigma, even to me," I said.

Josephs laughed. "Hey, you're in California, Mrs. Fletcher. Must have been the power of positive thinking that saved you. We're big into that out here. Mind over matter. A carrot juice once a day also helps. And plenty of sprouts."

"Or that dreadful sushi," said George.

"Do you have any suspects?" I asked.

Josephs shook his head. "None, Mrs. Fletcher. That's why I'm here. I was hoping you could give us more information. Like, maybe you've remembered something else about what happened." His eyes were hopeful.

My blank look burst his bubble. "I'm afraid I haven't had any flashbacks," I said. "Or psychic experiences, for that matter." My attempt at humor wasn't appreciated.

"Well, it was worth a shot," he said, finishing his drink. "I know one thing."

"Which is?" George asked.

"Some nut is running around San Fran pushing people off bridges. He's one for two. This guy Pearl didn't have his daily carrot juice like you, Mrs. Fletcher."

"I intend to start drinking it from this moment on," I said. "You said Brett Pearl's father identified the body."

"Right."

"Would you be good enough to give me his address and phone number?"

"Sure. I don't have it with me. Give me a call at the office in the morning."

"Thank you."

"You can tell me then what publisher you think should publish my novel."

"Tell you what, Detective Josephs," I said. "Instead of calling you, I'll come by your office and spend a few hours looking at the Kimberly Steffer files. We can talk about your book then."

"Yeah. Okay. I can arrange that. Make it eleven."

"I'll be there on the button."

As Josephs was leaving the suite, George Sutherland caught up with him at the door. I smiled as I heard him say, "Two things, Detective Josephs: One, you owe Mrs. Fletcher for the drink. Two, don't ever enter her room again without her prior permission."

"Hey, lighten up, George."

"I believe the drink is five dollars."

"Five dollars? I had a thimble full."

"Five dollars."

Josephs handed him the money.

"And did I make myself clear about not entering her room?"

Josephs laughed. It was forced. "You Scotch are some strange breed."

"Scotch is a whiskey, Detective. I am Scottish. A Scotsman. Good evening."

Chapter Eleven

Considering everything that had happened to me that day, I slept peacefully and awoke rested. I dressed in my favorite jumpsuit, a subtle pink affair, and sneakers. After a bountiful breakfast of eggs, bacon, sourdough bread, and fresh-squeezed orange juice at New Dawn, a café touted to me by Camille Inken as having the city's best breakfast, I waited on the corner for the Powell–Hyde Line cable car to rumble to a stop. I hadn't taken a cable-car ride in years. My destination was unclear. But that's the beauty of San Francisco's cable cars. You pay your fare and can jump on and off at random (especially if you're wearing a jumpsuit). I purchased a ticket that allowed me unlimited transfers for a three-hour period. Just in case I decided to keep riding until it was time for my eleven o'clock meeting with Detective Josephs.

I'd managed to read most of his partially completed manuscript before falling asleep, and finished it over breakfast. To be kind, it was dreadful. I never knew so many four-letter words existed in our language. The most popular of obscenities seemed to be used as an adjective for every other word in the text.

My reaction to what he'd written posed a dilemma for me, one that I've assiduously tried to avoid throughout my professional life. Agreeing to read what someone else has written places a large burden on the reader. What if you don't like it? What do you say? I've come up with a standard reply, so to speak, that combines gentleness with honesty. But it's awkward, at best.

Especially, when you want something in return, in this case sustained time with the Kimberly Steffer files at MPD. That necessitated being less than honest with Detective Josephs. Calculating on my part? Absolutely. But as my darling deceased father was fond of saying, "Necessity is the mother of invention." I'd be gently honest with Josephs *after* perusing the files. Until then, I'd be creative in how I deflected his questions about my response to his manuscript.

And so armed with my *MUNI San Francisco Street and Transit Map* in case I got lost, I set out for a few hours of happy cable-car sight-seeing.

Yesterday's ripple of heat that seemed to surprise the natives was still with us. But nothing like what I'd left back home in Cabot Cove. The newspaper and the TV weathermen reported that the insufferable heat over the Eastern Seaboard, held in place by stationary high pressure near Bermuda—a classic "Bermuda High"—had broken all records, not only for temperatures, but for the length of time it had gripped the region. Compared to Maine, Northern California's minor-league heat wave was winter-like. The humidity was low, and the sun disappeared frequently behind a collage of puffy clouds.

San Francisco is one of those rare cities that looks as good up close as it does from hundreds of feet above while making a final approach into San Francisco International Airport. Adding to the city's natural physical attractiveness is its people. They seem to mirror the rough-and-tumble, freewheeling history of the city, its gold rush days, its open society that has kept it in the forefront of social change. San Francisco's citizens also, it seems to me, reflect the sort of happiness that comes with living in a physically beautiful place.

I held on tight as I hung off the steps of the cable car. We came into another stop, where a knot of tourists, heavy video cameras swinging from their necks and pulling their heads forward, waited to board. To my surprise, I saw a familiar face in the crowd. Camille Inken spotted me at the same time, and her face lit up with a large smile. She climbed on next to me. "Jessica! What a surprise," she said, managing to give me a hug before the car lurched forward. "I've been wondering how you've been doing. In fact, I left a message on your voice mail a little bit ago. I would have called sooner, but I knew you were anxious for some R and R, and didn't need intrusions."

"Don't be silly," I said. "Sorry I missed your call

this morning. I got an early start. I had breakfast at a marvelous small restaurant. The coffee they serve is out of this world. The guidebooks are right. You folks here take your coffee as seriously as your Napa Valley wines."

"You should have called me," Camille said. "I would have joined you. I didn't have any breakfast plans."

"Actually, it was a last-minute decision. The dining room at the hotel is excellent, but I wanted to get out in the city, eat where the locals do."

"I understand," she said. "I called this morning for several reasons. Besides wondering how you were doing on your mini-holiday, I wanted to ask a favor."

"Oh?"

"I don't want to put you on the spot, although I suppose that's exactly what I'm doing. Don't feel bad if you want to say 'no.' "

"Okay."

"I have a niece, Rhet, of whom I'm very fond. We have a close, loving relationship. Anyway, she's a sophomore in high school, and believe it or not, she's interested in going into public relations, or something along those lines. Her high school is pretty progressive. It actually has a class in PR, and Rhet's enrolled in it. One of the things required of her is to coordinate a mock event. I took her to dinner last night because I had to review a god-awful place called 'What's to Eat?' outside of Sausalito, for a new publication, a local parents' newspaper. It's one of those restaurants kids love and parents hate. It's been around awhile."

"Yes, I've heard of it," I said, making a mental note to pursue it further with Camille at a later date. Maybe she picked up on something I'd missed, especially if she got to meet Mark Steffer's former partner, Bob Frederickson.

"Anyway," Camille continued, "the place is too young even for Rhet, but I think she secretly enjoyed it. The reason I mention it to you, Jessica, is that during dinner, Rhet asked me for some help in her assignment. I had the brilliant idea that maybe she could coordinate an appearance by you at her school. I know you're only in town for another couple of days, and I told her this. She said she could work fast to set it up. She's a real mover and shaker."

"PR in her blood," I said.

Camille laughed, and shrugged.

"Say no more," I said. "I'll do it. I always enjoy helping young people get started in their careers."

As the cable car slowed down, Camille said, "My stop. Jessica, you're wonderful. I'll make it up to you. How about dinner tonight? I've got an assignment to review another restaurant. It's been around for a long time, too, but hasn't been reviewed for a while. It just went through a renovation. I always bring guests. All the more people to try different dishes. I'd love it if you could make it. Won't you say yes?"

I didn't hesitate to accept her invitation. George Sutherland was committed to dinner with colleagues.

He'd asked me to join them but I'd declined, although we did arrange to touch base later in the evening.

"I'd love to, Camille. I don't have any plans."

"Reservations are at seven-thirty. I'll pick you up at the hotel at seven."

I watched as Camille nimbly hopped off and walked down the street, her stride strong and purposeful, a professional woman knowing where she was going, and how to get there. Her life, it appeared to me, revolved around her career, as it does with so many women these days. I was happy she had a loving relationship with her niece to balance things a bit.

I was flattered to be asked to do her niece a favor. But then it occurred to me that I'd have to speak to her high school class about *something*. What would that be? I knew one thing. I would not talk about journal writing. The last thing I needed was for some prepubescent teenager's diary to be planted in my bag.

I was having so much fun riding the cable cars around town that I almost forgot my appointment with Detective Josephs. I ran into police headquarters at five past eleven and asked the officer at the lobby desk for him. He phoned Josephs. "Third floor, ma'am," he said.

Josephs was waiting when the elevator doors opened. "Hello, there, Mrs. Fletcher. I was beginning to wonder whether you'd forgotten."

"Oh, no," I said. "Just too enamored of your beautiful city. I've been cable car hopping."

"You can get arrested for that."

"Why?"

"Cable car hopping. Fare beating."

"Oh, I wasn't—maybe 'hopping' was the wrong word."

"I knew what you meant. Come on."

I followed him to his office and sat down in a chair he pulled out for me.

"I'm glad you came by, Mrs. Fletcher. We've been getting some leads, although most aren't panning out. But some are pretty interesting."

"That's good to hear."

"First, Brett Pearl's death is now ruled a homicide."

"I don't see how it could be considered anything else."

"Yeah. He was a children's book illustrator. Correct?"

"Correct."

"You know him, Mrs. Fletcher?"

"No. Kimberly Steffer did."

Josephs leaned back in his chair. I thought he might tip over.

"He illustrated a few of her books," I said. "And then he sued her. He claimed that because her books had done well, he deserved more money than he'd originally contracted for."

"How do you know all this, Mrs. Fletcher?"

"A friend of mine wrote about the case. Besides,

my other friend, George Sutherland, did some investigating of the case on the British end."

"Your friend, George, has a nasty streak."

"No he doesn't."

"I didn't appreciate the way he talked to me when I was leaving your suite."

"He was protecting my interests."

"Lovers?"

"Lovers? George and me? Of course not. Just good friends."

"Hey, Mrs. Fletcher, don't kid a kidder. I pick up on those things. That's what I'm paid for."

"Then I have to say you're being overpaid, Detective Josephs."

He held up his hands in mock defense. "Okay, Mrs. Fletcher, don't get your dander up. So, what do you think of my book?"

"Your book. Yes. I read it last night with great interest. It is—interesting. Yes, definitely interesting."

"Hey, that's great. You'll give it to your publisher?"

"I, ah—I really need time to read it again. I read it fast. Skimmed it, you might say. I always skim something the first time. Then I go back to pick up the—finer—details. The subtle things."

"Sure. That's the way to do it."

"You're aware that Kimberly Steffer has dual citizenship," I said quickly, happy to change the subject. "British and American."

"Yes, I know that."

"Brett Pearl was also British."

"That's right."

"My *friend*, George Sutherland, became involved in the case when Kimberly's parents contacted him in London. George tried to interview Brett Pearl at Kimberly's parents' urging. But Pearl wasn't very cooperative."

"I see," said Josephs. "How long do you plan to stay in San Francisco?"

"Through the weekend. George and I—my friend, Detective Sutherland, and I plan to take some time to enjoy the city. We also thought we'd take a ride into the wine country. I've never been. I understand it's lovely."

"Yeah. Take plenty of bread and cheese. All the wine tastings can get you crocked unless you've got something in your stomach."

"Good advice. Now, you said you could arrange for me to spend some time with the Kimberly Steffer files. I'm ready to get started."

"Bad time, Mrs. Fletcher."

"But you said—"

"I know, I know. But the only way I can do it is sub rosa, off the books as they say. Unofficial. Too many brass around this morning."

"That's very disappointing," I said. "I came here specifically for that purpose."

"Have to be another day, Mrs. Fletcher. Sorry. Look, while you're in San Francisco, I think you should have protection."

"Police protection?"

"Right. Hate to have anything happen to a famous mystery writer on my watch."

"Oh, Detective Josephs, that isn't necessary, I assure you. After all, I have one of Scotland Yard's finest to protect me from harm."

I knew the minute I said it that I shouldn't have. Josephs' smirk confirmed it. "Where's he staying?" he asked. "At the Mark?"

"Yes. Where the conference is."

"I thought he might have moved over to the St. Francis."

His implication was annoying, but I said nothing.

"So, how long before you read my book again? You know, to pick up on the subtle points."

"Hard to say, Detective. My schedule is pretty booked up for the rest of my stay here. I'll have to find some—unofficial time."

Had he gotten my meaning? That two could play at the game of putting off what the other wanted? He toyed with a paper clip he'd straightened out. After a few moments of silence, he placed his hands flat on his desk and pushed himself up from his chair. "Okay, Mrs. Fletcher. Thanks for stopping by. My advice is for you to enjoy the city and the Napa Valley, tool around with your Scotch buddy, Sutherland, and stay out of the Kimberly Steffer case. What happened to you on the bridge is cause for concern. And now with this Brett Pearl's murder, I think your best bet is a low profile. Play tourist, not detective."

"He's Scottish," I said. "Scotch is a whiskey. And yes, Detective, I hear you."

"Come on," he growled.

"Where?"

"Your hotel. I'll drive you."

"I thought you were on duty."

"I am. Duty means protecting our citizens and visitors. I'll give you a lift."

He left the office, and I followed. We got in his unmarked car and headed for the St. Francis. As he drove, I took out a small notebook I always carry with me and made a note to phone the prison as soon as I got back to my room, to arrange to visit Kimberly Steffer. She'd probably read about her former illustrator's death plunge from the Golden Gate, and I wanted her reaction to it, hopefully to learn more about Brett Pearl and the legal action he'd brought against her.

As we approached the hotel, it was obvious that something unusual was afoot. There were television remote trucks parked in front; a swarm of what appeared to be press clogged the sidewalk. My first thought was that a famous person had checked in. The hotel has been known since its opening in 1904 as the focal point of San Francisco's celebrity set. On any given day, its twelve hundred rooms and suites might house a visiting head of state, a film star, or a Washington bigwig.

But as I exited the car, the sinking realization that the press was waiting for *me* hit my stomach like a Greek pastry.

"There she is," someone shouted. The flock headed in my direction. Cameras flashed, and eager journalists, their beaks open wide as if mother bird had just come back, squawked questions at me as I tried to find an eye in the mass through which to thread myself. Josephs saw what was happening and flashed his badge: "Back off," he yelled. "Let her through."

A narrow alley opened, and I moved quickly through it, with Josephs leading the way. The moment we passed through the doors and into the lobby, I saw George Sutherland standing at the reception desk. He stood on tiptoe and waved. Josephs and I went to him. I looked back over my shoulder. The press had stampeded through the doors and were closing in fast. Josephs turned and held up his hands, one holding his badge. I took advantage of the barrier he formed to ask George why he was there. As far as I knew, it was the final day of the conference at the Mark Hopkins, and he was to make a speech.

"I came the minute I heard the news on the telly," he said.

"What news?"

"About the attempt on your life. On the bridge."

"It was on television?" I said incredulously.

"Afraid so, Jessica. They played it up big. Network, I think."

"Network? They'll see it back in Cabot Cove."

"Possibly."

"Probably is more like it."

With the press held at bay, Josephs turned to us. "You responsible for this?" he asked George.

"Don't be daft."

"Gorry, what a mess," I said.

"What?" said Josephs.

"She's from Maine," George said. "Come on, Jessica. Let's get upstairs." He took my elbow, and we made it to the doors of the outdoor glass elevators that provide its passengers a spectacular view of the city. An open door beckoned and we got in. With Josephs again protecting our rear, the doors closed, shutting out the clamoring members of the Fourth Estate.

As we ascended—I wasn't in any mood to appreciate the view—I said angrily, "I cannot believe this. I wanted a quiet few days here. Not a media circus. Not to have every move I make scrutinized by a pack of reporters."

The elevator stopped on Thirty-one, and the doors opened. "Come on," George said. "My room is this way."

"*Your* room?" I said.

Without another word, he led Josephs and me down the hall and into another suite adjoining my Windsor Suite. It was smaller than mine but equally as handsome.

"This is your room?" Josephs said.

"Certainly is," George said.

"What happened to the Mark Hopkins?" I asked.

"Not as of this morning, Jessica. Seeing the story on the telly made up my mind. The last straw, you might say. I called, booked this room, and moved right over. This door connects to your second—empty—bedroom," he said, directing it at Josephs.

"George, it wasn't necessary for you to—"

Josephs gave me an infuriating wink and smile.

"I don't believe this, George," I said. "This is a nightmare. What about your speech?"

"Already gave it. Breakfast speaker. Best time. Everyone's relatively awake. Went quite well, actually."

"You didn't need this, either," I said.

The phone rang.

"Let it ring," George said.

The message light was flashing furiously. I picked up the phone. A recorded voice told me I'd received twenty-one calls, and that there was no more room on the tape for messages.

"Don't mind me," Josephs said as he went to the bar and poured himself an orange juice. He turned on the TV, tuned in a local channel on which the news was playing, and plopped into a chair. After one of two anchors reported on a robbery in Oakland that resulted in a store owner being killed, my face lit up the screen. It was a photograph that had been provided by my publisher for my publicity tour.

The anchor handed it over to a reporter: ". . . *Live at the Westin St. Francis where Mrs. Fletcher is staying.*"

"*Thank you, Wally. I'm here in the hotel lobby where Jessica Fletcher, America's favorite mystery writer, has just arrived. She was escorted by a detective from the MPD, and they've gone upstairs, pre-*

sumably to Mrs. Fletcher's suite, accompanied by another man. According to what we've learned, an attempt was made on her life yesterday when an unidentified assailant tried to push her off the Golden Gate. I've also learned—and this is based upon unconfirmed reports—that while Mrs. Fletcher came to San Francisco ostensibly to hype her latest novel, her real reason was to reopen a murder case from the past, the murder of restaurateur Mark Steffer. Steffer, you might recall, owned a restaurant in Sausalito, What's To Eat? His wife, noted children's book author Kimberly Steffer, was convicted of that crime, and is currently serving time in the Women's Correctional Facility. That's about it from here, Wally. I'll be standing by in case there are further developments. Back to you."

"The nerve," I said. "I came here to promote my book. Getting involved with Kimberly Steffer was an accident."

"I know," George said. "Bloody press. The Italians call them *Rapaces*. Ghoulish vultures."

"I know," I said. "I bumped into Camille Inken this morning. She's the publicity gal who handled my San Francisco tour. I'm having dinner with her tonight. I'll call her now. She should know how to put this to rest. To give me—*us* some rest. If she thinks it's necessary, we can hold a press conference. Whatever it takes. Just as long as it results in peace and quiet."

"Any idea how this got out?" asked George.

"No."

"Perhaps it was this Camille person."

"Camille? No. She wouldn't do such a thing to me."

Josephs guffawed from where he continued to sit in front of the TV. "Don't be so sure, Mrs. Fletcher. Those publicity types will do anything to get a name in the paper." He jumped up and added, "Hey, this is great for your book. Should sell out all over town. All over the country if the news is on the networks."

I ignored him, and the temptation to call him *Rapaces*. I said to George, "It couldn't be Camille. I never even told her about any of this. I was planning on doing that tonight. Of course, she knows now, thanks to our reporter friends."

"I told Mrs. Fletcher I'd like to provide security for her while she's in San Fran," said Detective Josephs. "With all this media attention, it makes even more sense. You agree, George?"

"Frankly," replied George, speaking to me, "I think you should put yourself on the first available plane and go home. Get away from here."

My reaction was anger, and I knew my expression mirrored it. It wasn't George's suggestion that caused it. It was the scenario that had caused him to offer it.

"I'm not leaving," I said flatly. "The news just broke. Things will quiet down by tomorrow. They'll move on to bigger and better stories."

"Don't count on it, Jess," George said. He turned to Josephs, who'd sat in the chair again and was intently watching a sports report. "Detective Josephs, I wonder if you'd be good enough to leave Mrs. Fletcher and me alone."

Josephs stood. "Kickin' me out, huh? It's okay. I still say you should have round-the-clock protection, Mrs. Fletcher. But that's your call. I suppose you don't need it with Scotland Yard on the case."

"Your offer is very kind, Detective," I said, "but not necessary. I'll call the moment I've had a chance to read your manuscript again. Maybe we can get together then, and I can spend a few hours with your computer."

"Why don't you drop that, Mrs. Fletcher. Forget Kimberly Steffer. Go off to the wine country and hide out. Drink wine. Remember to bring cheese and bread."

"Cheese and bread?" George said.

"I'll explain," I said. "Again, thank you, Detective. We'll be in touch."

Josephs gave me one of his annoying smirks, and winked at George. "Have fun, folks." He left.

"As we say in Scotland, a thoroughly *fousome* man," George said. "Most disagreeable."

"George."

"Yes?"

"You do know how much I appreciate everything you're doing for me."

"I've done nothing."

"Moving over here to the St. Francis, listening to me, understanding me."

"I only wish we had more time together, Jessica, to develop that understanding." We stood close to each other. I looked into his green eyes, gentle, kind eyes as I remembered them being the first time we met in London, over tea at Brown's Hotel. Even though he'd been interrogating me at the time, and had actually considered me a possible suspect in the murder of my dear friend and reigning queen of mystery writing, Dame Marjorie Ainsworth, he was kind and considerate.

"I would like that, too, George," I said, averting my gaze and pretending to rearrange books that didn't need rearranging.

"You might have noticed, Jessica, that I'm quite fond of you."

I continued to focus on the books. He came up behind me and said, "I know I'm not the most handsome of men. Nor am I the success that you are. I am just a copper. But I sense a certain kinship between us. It's the sort of feeling I haven't enjoyed since my wife died so many years ago."

I turned. "George," I said, "you are a very handsome man. And you are a great success. I would be less than honest if I didn't admit to strong feelings for you, too. A kinship, as you put it. But we really don't know much about each other. We really don't know each other at all."

"You make my point exactly, Jessica. All I'm suggesting is that we create the opportunity to get to know each other better. It might turn out that familiarity truly does breed contempt. But I rather think it won't. I think of you a great deal, Jessica, as I sit in my office, or take a holiday at what was my family's home in Wick. And when I do, I can't help but recite Robbie Burns to myself."

I smiled. "And what did Robert Burns write that I remind you of?"

"A small ditty. A tribute to his wife. Let me see: *'Of a' the airts the wind can blaw, I dearly like the west, For there the bonnie Lassie lives, The Lassie I lo'e best.'* "

"That's—that's very touching, George."

"Ah, good old Robbie Burns. Putting into words what we feel, but cannot say."

He placed his hands on my shoulders and looked deep into my eyes. His lips came close to mine. I took a breath, and closed my eyes.

The phone's first ring sounded as though it had been magnified a thousand times. It jolted my eyes open, and caused me to flinch.

"Just another reporter," said George.

"Hello," I said quietly.

"Jessica?"

"Yes."

"Jessica, what on earth is going on?"

"Oh, hello Mort. Nice to hear your voice. Your timing is—wonderful."

"It is?"

"Yes. You caught me here. I was going out. How are you?"

"Jessica Fletcher, you cut it out right now. We've got reporters crawlin' out of the woodwork here. They keep sayin' you flew back home today. Did you?"

"I don't think so, Mort. You reached me here in San Francisco."

"I know that. I got confused for a minute. You've got some explainin' to do, young lady."

"Why, for heaven's sake?"

" 'Cause you can't keep people in the dark like you've been doin'."

I laughed. "Oh, Mort, take it easy."

"Easy for you to say."

"If the press believes I flew home today, so much the better. Makes for a quieter and more peaceful time for me here."

His exasperated sigh blew in my ear. "At least I know you're alive. Been gettin' calls from damn near everybody here in Cabot Cove. Whole town saw the news on TV."

"Yes, I'm very much alive, Mort, and feeling just fine, thank you."

"You sound all right. If you didn't, I'd be on the next plane to Frisco."

"I don't think San Franciscans like to have their city called 'Frisco,' Mort. But I know you'd be here in a flash. It's sweet of you to care that much."

"I've done it before. Remember?"

"Oh, yes, I certainly do remember." Fortunately, he couldn't see me wince at the memory.

"Jessica, is there any truth to this business about you bein' pushed off the Golden Gate Bridge?"

"I'm afraid so, Mort, although I wasn't pushed off. I hung on for dear life. I was taking a walk across the bridge, and someone tried to shove me off. Fortunately, didn't succeed. I'm fine. Not a bruise or a bump. Except to my psyche."

"Did they get the guy?"

"No. Or the gal. They have no suspects at this time."

"So why are you bein' so darned jo-jeezly, Jessica? Get out of there and come home. That crazy city's no place for you to be hangin' around. They got more crazies out there per square inch than a nuthouse."

"It's a wonderful city, Mort. I love it here. Almost as much as Cabot Cove. And I intend to stay for a few more days and have a real vacation. Please don't worry. I can take care of myself. Besides, George Sutherland is here to keep an eye on me."

There was silence on the other end.

"So what do I tell these reporters?" he finally said.

"Good question," I said. "I'll tell you what. I'm having dinner tonight with my publicist, Camille Inken. She's terrific at what she does. I'll ask her advice and let you know what she says."

"You say George Sutherland is with you?"

"Yes. In fact, he's right here at the moment. Want to say hello?"

"Maybe another time. You aren't thinkin' of—?"

"Of what, Mort?"

"Of gettin' involved with him."

"Ah, no—maybe. Wouldn't that be nice?"

"Depends. I don't have a lot of trust in Limeys."

"George is from Scotland."

"Scotch, either."

I didn't bother correcting him.

"They all sound good when they talk—real cultured and all that—but that doesn't mean you can trust 'em. I read about all those sex scandals they have every day over there. Pretty important people, too."

"Mort, I really have to run. I'll talk to Camille tonight and call you first thing in the morning."

"Okay, Jess, but hurry it up. And watch yourself with this Sutherland fella."

"I certainly will. Say hello to everyone, and tell them I'm alive and kicking."

I hung up and looked at George, who stood at the window, a bemused smile on his lips.

"Sorry," I said, "I have a call to make."

"Would you like me to leave?"

"Of course not. Not a personal call. In fact, it occurs to me that I might be able to coerce you into joining forces with me."

"Sounds intriguing."

I dialed the operator. "This is Jessica Fletcher. I'd like the number for the Women's Correctional Facility in Oakland."

I glanced up at George, whose response was to lower himself into a chair and to slowly shake his head.

I dialed the number given me. "Hello," I said. "I'd like to inquire about visiting an inmate this afternoon. Her name is Kimberly Steffer. I've visited her before. My name is Jessica Fletcher. I believe I'm included on the list of visitors she'll see." He consulted the list, confirmed I was on it, and gave me the visiting hours.

"Thank you, sir. I'll be there."

George joined me on the couch. "I know, I know," I said. "I'm a *dour* woman."

"Yes, you are, Jessica. And worse. Of course I'll accompany you. You might as well get used to the fact that I intend to be at your side every moment we have together in this jewel of a city. I only ask that we stay off bridges, and do our level best to avoid that annoying Detective Josephs."

I couldn't help but giggle. "Not long ago, when I was in New York promoting another of my books, *Manhattans and Murder*—I believe I sent you a copy—I had to disguise myself in order to buy some peace and quiet. Silly wig, big sunglasses. I looked like a fool. A real lumper's helper, as we say back home. When that adventure was over, I pledged that I would never put myself through such nonsense again. So, George, if you see me in a wig and over-size sunglasses, you have my permission to put on the straitjacket, and physically place me on a plane back east."

"Fair enough." He kissed me on the cheek and stood. "Where to first?" he asked, grinning.

Chapter Twelve

"Thank you for coming again," Kimberly Steffer said. Her tone was solemn.

"How are you doing?"

"Okay, I guess."

"This gentleman with me is Detective Sergeant George Sutherland. He's with Scotland Yard in London, and did some investigating in your case there."

"Pleased to meet you," she said in her British accent. "I've heard your name. I believe you tried to help me."

"Without much success, I'm afraid," George said. There had been a few minutes of tension when we'd arrived at the facility because George's name wasn't on Kimberly's list of approved visitors. But his credentials, which he proudly displayed, and a call to Kimberly, did the trick.

"Kimberly," I said, "I assume you've heard that Brett Pearl is dead."

She studied my face. Her soft, round eyes narrowed. "No, I didn't know that. I don't keep up with the news in here. How did Brett die?"

His body was found yesterday floating beneath the Golden Gate Bridge."

"Oh, my God," she said, her hands covering her mouth. "That's awful." She paused. "But I'm not surprised. Brett was depressed a lot. He had that sort of personality. Downbeat. Seeing the worst in things. Brett's glass was always half empty. But he was talented. Very talented."

"He didn't commit suicide, Kimberly. The police have ruled his death a homicide."

"Homicide? You mean someone caused him to fall from the bridge?"

"Looks that way."

"Any suspects yet?" Kimberly seemed to ask it more out of curiosity than concern.

"None, as far as I know."

"I'm sorry to hear that," she said, her voice void of emotion.

I didn't know the extent of their relationship, although considering his lawsuit against her, I presumed it wasn't especially cordial. From her reaction, I'd say I was right.

"There's more," I said. "I was nearly pushed off the bridge shortly before Brett Pearl's body was discovered."

"What?" She said it loud enough for the guard to look over. "What happened?" she whispered, leaning in.

I kept my voice low. "I was taking a walk across the bridge when suddenly, out of nowhere, someone grabbed hold of me and tried to push me over. Fortunately, I managed to hang on."

"How terrible. Are you okay?"

"Yes, I'm fine. Still a little shaken by the experience whenever I think of it, but otherwise okay."

"I'm so sorry," she said. "It obviously had to do with me, and the fact you've gotten involved with me."

"Perhaps. There's something else I need to tell you."

I recounted my confrontation with Ellie's godmother. As I spoke, she became visibly upset. Her mouth tightened, and her eyes narrowed into angry slits.

When I was finished, she spoke in a firm, controlled voice. "I worry so about Ellie because of Joan, even though Nancy has virtual custody of her. Joan has an enormous influence over her—after all, she is her real mother—and Ellie loves her. That's understandable. But Joan is an evil and sick woman. Mark knew better than anyone what she was really, truly like, although I've had my share of encounters with her to attest to her wickedness."

"Wicked enough to have killed Mark?" George asked.

Kimberly frowned. "I've always suspected that she had *something* to do with Mark's death, Detective Sutherland. I'm certainly not claiming that she pulled the trigger. I could never prove that, of course. I suppose that's why I'm sitting here talking to you through this piece of breath-stained Plexiglas.

Hoping you—both of you?—might find proof that I didn't have anything to do with it."

I asked, "Do you have any idea who might have wanted Brett Pearl dead? Did Joan know him? Nancy Antonio?"

"I don't think so. I really don't know, except that it wouldn't have been through my introduction. His name is on some of my books, so they could have 'known' him that way."

"Did Mark ever have a run-in with him?"

"Yes. Absolutely. You know that Brett sued me because the books we worked on together sold much better than anyone could have forecast. Mark was furious about the suit, and let Brett know it. Mark was, after all, my husband."

"Of course," I said, noticing delicate tears form in her eyes.

She sniffled. "Jessica, we may have not had a marriage made in heaven, but we had many pleasant things going for us. Mark wasn't always *by* my side. He worked hard, long hours, and used what little free time he had to play golf." She managed a small smile. "Which made me the classic golf widow. But he was always *on* my side. I took considerable comfort from that."

"I understand," I said.

The guard signaled that our time was up.

"We have to leave, Kimberly. But we'll be back." I glanced at George, who nodded. "I can't say for sure just when, but it will be within the next few days."

Which meant, I knew, having to extend my "vacation" in San Francisco. George, too.

"Jessica, wait," Kimberly said. She spoke rapidly and softly; I strained to hear her. "There is someone you might want to talk to about Brett's death. Brett had a best friend by the name of Norman Lana. They were roommates for a spell. Brett never married. This roommate, Norman, was an odd chap. Mark never trusted him. No real reason for it. He just had a hunch about him. Norman supposedly had a dreadful temper. It's funny because, to tell you the truth, I'd always found him to be pleasant. I actually enjoyed his company, even though we never spent much time together. He'd occasionally join us for a drink, that sort of thing. Norman was a lively, animated sort of fellow. I always suspected he was gay, but he never confirmed that to me. He was fun to be around.

"But after Mark's death, I've thought a lot about Norman Lana. Not just fleeting thoughts. I've wondered if he, somehow, for some reason, might have been involved in the murder."

"Time's up, ma'am," the prison guard said.

"Better go," Kimberly said. "I don't want to be in trouble. It's hard enough here without angering them."

"Of course," I said. It was obvious that Kimberly had her eye set on an early release for good behavior. Better yet, for wrongful imprisonment, I thought as George and I left the visitation room.

*　　*　　*

I was pleased to see that the TV remote trucks were gone when we pulled up in front of the St. Francis. We entered the lobby and were heading for the elevators when Camille Inken's voice stopped me.

"Camille. What are you doing here?" I asked.

"Checking up on my favorite author, that's what. I heard the news. *Everyone* has heard the news. What a dreadful thing that happened to you, Jessica. Thank God you're all right."

"Oh, yes, I'm fine. Camille. This is Detective-Inspector George Sutherland. Scotland Yard in London. We're friends."

"A pleasure," said Camille, shaking his hand.

"The pleasure is mine, Ms. Inken. I've heard nothing but good things about you from Mrs. Fletcher."

"Happy to hear that," Camille said.

"Who are those chaps over there?" George asked.

We looked in the direction he'd indicated, where several very large men in suits, and who had "bodyguard" written all over them, roamed the lobby. Their coiled earplugs did nothing to dash my evaluation of them.

"Bodyguards to protect the prince of some country or other," Camille said. "I asked the manager about them. I forget the prince's name. His country, too, for that matter."

"Where is the press?" I asked.

"Lucky you, Jess," Camille said. "The prince is checking in this afternoon. One of the conditions for his stay here is that all press be barred from the hotel."

"That's good news," said George. "But there aren't any reporters lurking outside, either."

Camille beamed. "I took care of that," she said.

"How?" I asked.

"They think you've left town. I spread the word that you were flying back to Boston this morning. Unofficially, of course. By now, the airport should be overrun with them."

"Bravo, Camille," George said.

"But I don't promise anything if we keep standing here in the lobby," Camille said.

We went to my suite, fixed ourselves cold drinks, and sat in the living room.

"I spoke to Rhet, Jessica," Camille said. "As you can imagine, she's thrilled, absolutely thrilled that you've offered to speak. She's in the throes of organizing the event. Is Friday okay with you? At ten? I need to phone her tonight to let her know."

"Looks like I'll still be in San Francisco," I said. "Sure. Friday at ten sounds fine."

"Perhaps you'd like to join us," she said to George.

I explained why I'd be going to the high school.

"Delighted," he said. "Provided I'm not required to do anything like making a speech."

"That's a promise," Camille said.

"Would you excuse me for a few minutes?" George asked.

"Where are you going?" I asked.

"To send a fax to the office. I think I'd better inform them that my return will be delayed for an unspecified period of time."

"Sure that's all right?" I asked.

"No problem, Jessica. Be back in a jiffy."

When he was gone, Camille raised her eyebrows, and made the circular okay sign with her thumb and index finger. "What a doll," she said.

"George? A delightful man."

"You—?"

"No. Just a friend. A very *good* friend."

"Uh-huh. How about having him join us for dinner tonight?"

"I think he's committed."

"Too bad. I'd get a kick out of chaperoning you two."

"We don't need a chaperon."

"Uh-huh."

George returned and accepted our dinner invitation. He'd "cleared the decks" for the rest of his stay in San Francisco, including his dinner plans that evening.

"Great," Camille said. "I've got to be running along. A million things to do before I pick you up for dinner. See you two at seven?"

"We'll be waiting," George said.

"Now, Jessica, if anyone disturbs you—any member of the press—refer the call or inquiry to me," Camille said as she poised at the door. "I know most of them. Believe me, they're a harmless bunch. See you tonight."

"Lovely woman," said George as he sat on the couch.

"And very efficient. Can I fix you a drink?"

"Thank you, no. I'm sleepy enough as it is. Would you mind if I stretched out for a short nap in my new bedroom?"

"Of course not."

"By the way, Jessica, the prince's security entourage has been put on full alert. Seems he received a death threat."

"Oh?"

"Somewhat unsettling isn't it, staying in the same hotel in which someone has received a death threat?"

"Even more unsettling is to be staying in a hotel in which *two* people have received them. Especially when you're one of them."

"Yes. Shouldn't have brought it up. Wake me in an hour?"

"Count on it," I said.

Chapter Thirteen

It had started to pour in San Francisco as George
and I came down to the lobby to wait for Camille.
We stood at a front window and looked out over
the glistening street. People scrambled for cover beneath umbrellas, or newspapers held over their
heads.

"There she is, George."

We ran through the rain to a silver-gray Lincoln
Continental that pulled up to the curb. Camille
opened the rear door and waved us in. She looked
ready for a splashy evening on the town. Her
makeup was perfect, her hair swept up into a chif-
fon, and she was draped in an elegant black silk
cape.

We tumbled into the car, our coats dripping water
onto the red leather seats.

"Sorry I didn't get out to help you," the driver
said over his shoulder.

"I would have questioned your sanity if you had,"
I replied.

He laughed. "Where to, Ms. Inken?"

"Coit Tower, please." To us: "I thought you might like to share one of my favorite sights."

"Hardly a night for sight-seeing," George said.

"*Perfect* night for seeing *this* sight," said Camille. "It's spectacular in the sun, but even more breathtaking in the rain."

"Sounds like what a Scotsman might say," I said, squeezing George's arm.

"Ay. I've been *droukit* more than once back home."

"Droukit?" Camille and I said in unison.

"Soaking wet. We do get a wee bit of rain now and then where I come from."

"Where is your home?" Camille asked.

"A place in Scotland you've probably never heard of," George replied. "A small town far north called Wick."

"Near John o' Groat's," Camille said.

"Right you are, Ms. Inken."

"I've been there. One of the most beautiful natural sights I've ever seen was in Wick, Scotland. Right on the coast. I'll never forget it. Or the horizontal rain."

George laughed. "It does tend to come at you in a funny way when the wind is blowing hard."

"Sounds intriguing," I said.

"But not enough for me to entice you to visit me there, Jessica," George said.

"Oh, you must go, Jess," Camille said.

"I'd love to but—"

"Work on her this evening, Ms. Inken. My family

home in Wick sits on a bluff overlooking the very sights you mention. Big house. Fourteen rooms, and all empty most of the year, 'cept for a caretaker and his wife. I rent it out to tourists now and then, but make sure it's empty when I visit."

Camille looked at me and raised her eyebrows into question marks. Her smile was knowing, almost wicked.

"One of these days," I said.

"That's progress," said George.

We parked near the famed Coit Tower, on top of Telegraph Hill, the first West Coast telegraph station that transmitted messages notifying the arrival of ships from the Pacific. The rain had let up sufficiently for us to get out of the limo, but the wind had picked up, not quite enough to create the "horizontal rain" of northern Scotland, but enough to whip the drizzle and fog into grotesque, eerie swirls of light and dark.

"Spectacular," I said, looking through the mist out over the bay and the city.

"Like Wick?" Camille asked George.

"Not quite, but close enough."

The heavens opened again, and we sought the warm, dry refuge of the limo. "Where to now?" I asked Camille.

"To eat."

As we headed back toward center city, Camille told me that her niece's assignment had changed at the last minute. "Her teacher felt it would be more fitting for a class in public relations to stage a mock press conference for you, Jess, instead of simply having you speak."

"Sounds like an interesting idea," I said.

"Rhet will schedule and handle a press conference at which you'll announce a motion picture deal for one of your books. A fake movie deal, of course."

"A shame it has to be fake," I said. "I could use a movie deal. It's been awhile."

"Speaking of press conferences, Jess, how did your sheriff friend back in Maine make out? Did he hold one like I suggested?"

I shook my head. "I called him right after you made that suggestion, but he decided issuing a written statement would suffice."

"What was he going to write?" asked George.

"Camille had a good suggestion, George. Tell them the truth, except the part about my still being in San Francisco. Tell them it was a frightful experience, that I took a vacation someplace else to recover, and that I wanted privacy."

"I like the last part best," George said. "I just wish the first part was true, that we'd—that you'd gone someplace else to get over it."

Our driver came to a stop, jumped out of the car, and came around to the back door carrying a large green-and-white golf umbrella. It was raining hard again as we got out and tried to huddle beneath the umbrella. It wasn't until we were standing directly in front of the restaurant that I realized where we were. The building's facade was elegant black marble. The door was bright gold. Of course. We were having dinner at Restaurant Isuzu, where George and I had dined the previous night. I looked back at George, who was too busy opening the door for us to notice where he was. We stepped inside and were being helped out of our raincoats when he laughed and said, "Well, what do you know."

Camille didn't hear him because she'd sought out the maître d' to inquire about our reservation. I whispered to George, "Let's not say anything."

He grinned and agreed.

The maître d' approached and said, "Mrs. Fletcher. What a pleasant surprise. So good to see you again so soon."

"You've been here before?" Camille asked.

"Yes," I answered sheepishly. "Last night. George and I had dinner."

"I'm sorry," Camille said. "If I'd known, I would have—"

"Not another word," I said. "George and I are very fond of sushi. Aren't we, George?"

"What? Oh, yes, indeed. Can't seem to get enough of it."

The host said, "I was disappointed last night, Mrs. Fletcher, that I failed to ask you if you would be so kind to pose for a picture that we could hang on the wall." He pointed behind us. "We think of it as our celebrity wall. Your photo would be a special treasure."

"After dinner," Camille snapped.

I didn't know whether she was annoyed at the photo request, or that we'd been at Restaurant Isuzu before. All I knew was that I was a lot more willing to honor this photo request than I'd been with Robert Frederickson at What's To Eat?.

As the maître d' took my arm, Camille said, "I'm really sorry to be bringing you back here."

"But I'm so glad we're back," I said. "The food is heavenly, and so is the service. We had a memorable meal." I didn't add that the previous night's dinner had sated my yearning for sushi for six months. Maybe a second helping so soon would result in a cumulative effect, lasting a year.

Camille and I ordered saki. George stayed with the same Japanese beer as the previous night. He lifted his glass to us and said, "To the joys of sushi, the staff of every Scotsman's life." We laughed and clinked rims. He turned to me. "Enjoy your silki, Jessica."

Chapter Fourteen

"Good morning, Jessica."

"Good morning, George."

"Wake you?"

"I was half awake. Now I'm all the way there."

"Lovely evening."

"Yes, it was. I hope two consecutive nights in a sushi restaurant won't permanently upset your digestive tract."

"Not at all. The tempura was as good second time around as it was first. Ready for our stroll?"

"What stroll?"

"Across the bridge. Splendid day for it."

"Across the bridge? The Golden Gate?"

"Yes."

"I thought you were joking when you suggested it last night."

"Hardly. I've never done it. You have. And I would welcome your expertise, as well as your companionship."

"George, I don't think I can—"

"You know, Jessica, when you fall off a bicycle, it's best to get right back on."

I laughed. "I'm well aware of that sage advice, George. But falling off a bike, and falling off the Golden Gate Bridge, are two very different things. A scraped knee from one. A watery death from the other."

"I promise that the worst thing will happen to you is a scraped knee. Well?"

"Get the bikes ready."

We met downstairs for a breakfast of sourdough croissants and tea, hailed a cab, and were soon standing at the San Francisco end of the soaring, majestic, rust-colored bridge. The weather was perfect. There was considerably less wind than the day of my first venture across the span.

"Ready?" asked George, a broad smile on his tanned, handsome face. He wore a Harris tweed jacket with leather patches at the elbows, tan twill slacks, shirt and tie, and sported a red scarf wrapped casually about his neck in the fashion of 1930s open cockpit aviators. His face was like that of a veteran pilot, too, deeply creased from having squinted for too many hours into a strong sun. His sunglasses had brown lenses, and gold wire frames.

I'd chosen to wear what I'd worn on my first jaunt across the bridge, ivory cable-knit sweater, sweatpants, sneakers, and red, white, and blue windbreaker.

"Yes," I said, trying to force my voice to sound confident. "Ready as I'll ever be."

"Then, off we go."

He set a quick pace—George was an avid walker back in London, always opting to use foot power rather than riding the double-decker buses, or using the city's famed black taxicabs. I huffed and puffed initially to keep up, but soon fell into his rhythm. The bright, warm sun polished my skin, the wind kissed my face. A feeling of euphoria came over me; the smile on my face was involuntary and pleased. Like the first time on the bridge.

We slowed our pace. George walked almost sideways so that he could admire the view as he went. I had trouble looking anywhere but straight ahead. I was afraid that if I looked out over the railing, I'd panic and have to call off our walk.

"Hard to imagine that one earthquake, one tremor, could wipe out all this beauty," George said into the wind.

"Not a pleasant contemplation," I replied, aware that the bridge was probably the worst place to be if an earthquake hit.

"Takes a bit of courage to live out here," he said.

"Depends on your philosophy," I said. "It's a perfect place for fatalists."

"Are you a fatalist, Jessica?"

"To an extent. I believe in taking charge of one's life. I don't believe in luck. I think we make our own luck. On the other hand, there are things beyond our control."

"Like an earthquake."

"Like an earthquake."

"Love?"

"Love? I'll have to think about that."

I started walking again. George caught up, and we continued at a leisurely gait.

"Jessica, I've been thinking," he said, grabbing my arm and bringing us to a halt.

I swallowed hard. My heart skipped. My legs felt weak. We'd reached the halfway point of our walk. We were mere yards from where I'd nearly been pushed off the bridge. I looked down to the glistening water and small boats bobbing about. It came back to me with the force of a horse's hoof to my stomach. I shuddered.

"Are you all right?" George asked. He saw that I wasn't, and embraced me.

"Look," he said. "The view is beautiful. Take a peek. I won't let anything happen to you."

I lifted my head slowly. Secure in the comfort of his strong arms, I turned to share his view of San Francisco's breathtaking skyline.

"From this vantage point, Jessica, everything seems possible. Wouldn't you agree?"

"Let's continue," I said.

"No. Let's stay here for a moment and talk."

"About?"

"At this lovely moment, I wish to say that I enjoy your company more than anyone I know. More than any woman I've met since my wife died. I think you are a wonderful woman, Jessica. I do hope you know that."

He looked down into my eyes and smiled.

"Well, I certainly know it now," I said, "although

I must admit I had a hunch about it the past few days."

"I suppose I have made it obvious," he said. "Not very subtle, I'm afraid."

I laughed. "Oh, no, George, a lot more subtle than most men I know. And I think you are very special, too. I trust *you* know that."

"I'd hoped you'd felt that way. What I'm getting at, Jessica, is that I think we should—"

"What *I* think, George, is that we'd better finish our walk and get off this bridge before there *is* an earthquake." I realized my comment could have been taken two ways. I also knew that he wouldn't make something of the second, corny interpretation.

He said, "Not so fast. We have precious few moments to talk like this. This is perfect. We're surrounded by beauty. We're alone. Well, sort of alone. And I haven't finished saying what I wish to say."

I waited.

"I've been thinking—Ms. Inken firmed my resolve last night—I've been thinking that it's time for you to visit me in Scotland."

"And I'd love that."

"Loving the idea, and acting upon it are two very different things, Jessica. I want you to make a commitment to come to Wick, and to stay in my family home for a few weeks. You could come for the Christmas holidays. Wick might not offer the same sort of festivities as your Cabot Cove, but it has its own special way of celebrating."

"I don't think I could be away from home at Christmas," I said.

"I seem to remember you recently spent a fateful Christmas in New York City."

He was right. I'd been there a few years ago on a book-promotion tour, and ended up deeply involved in murder and police corruption.

"I assure you Wick will be considerably less turbulent than New York City," he added.

"I don't doubt that for a moment."

A middle-aged couple passed, arm in arm.

"I'd love to visit you in Scotland," I said.

"Marvelous. I'll reserve your flight as soon as I return home."

"Let's walk," I said.

We hooked arms and continued in the direction of Marin County. George talked the entire way about what my visit to Wick would entail. Holiday parties with old friends, festive dinners with remaining members of his family, and time in London to take in some theater. The more he talked, the less ambivalent were my feelings about finally agreeing to make the trip. But I had strong mixed emotions. It would undoubtedly be a lovely experience, one I would treasure for the rest of my life. But there was the parallel feeling that to visit him there would force us together faster than I was ready for. Maybe I'd never be ready for another commitment to a man. Although my late husband had died years ago, I still felt a commitment to *him,* not in a ghoulish or warped sense; I was free to meet and marry someone else, literally and psychically. But whether that was in my future plans was something with which I'd not yet chosen to grapple.

We reached the other end of the bridge and walked through a parking lot to an overlook. It wasn't until we were practically on top of it that I noticed the marked San Francisco MPD squad car.

"Detective Josephs," I said. He was leaning on the rail looking out over the city and bay.

"Good morning, Mrs. Fletcher. Inspector."

George grunted a greeting.

"We must stop meeting like this, Mrs. Fletcher," Josephs said, tossing George a small smile.

"We just walked across the bridge," I said.

"Got back on the bike, huh?" said Josephs.

"You might say that. Mind if I ask what you're doing here? You're out of your territory."

"That's right. Pretty morning. Thought I'd drive over and take in the scenery."

"Anything new on the drowning?" George asked.

"Brett Pearl? No. Sometimes you get a fresh perspective on a case when you look at it from a different angle."

"From this side of the bridge, instead of the other?" I said.

"That's right, Mrs. Fletcher. Hey, by the way, did you get a chance to have a closer read of my book?"

"No. Sorry to say I haven't. But I will."

"Yeah. Well, whenever you get around to it." He asked George if he was having a good time in San Francisco.

"Very nice, Detective. Mrs. Fletcher is seeing to that."

"I bet she is." He returned his attention to the vista of city and sea, saying without looking at us, "We've determined that Pearl was pushed to his death between nine-ten and nine-fifteen. His body was discovered at nine-eighteen by a passerby in a boat. Which means he wasn't down there very long. Just a couple of minutes." He turned and faced me. "If I remember correctly, Mrs. Fletcher, you came into my office about nine-forty-five, give or take a few minutes. Let's say for argument's sake it took you half an hour to get to my office from the bridge. Fifteen minutes to get off the bridge, maybe ten, fifteen minutes in a cab. Add up?"

"Yes."

"Witnesses place Pearl walking in this direction. Toward Sausalito. The same direction you were headed that morning. I figure he got pushed off at just about the same spot where you almost got it. That means you probably passed him on your way back to city side. Are you following me?"

"Yes, I think so. But I don't see the relevance of what you're saying. Suppose I did pass him. What would that mean?"

Josephs shrugged. "Could mean you knew he was going to be there."

"But I didn't know he was going to be there. I didn't know *him*."

"I've got somebody says you *did* know him, Mrs. Fletcher."

"And who might that be?" George asked.

"A confidential source."

"I assume you've heard of the decent concept of allowing citizens to face their accusers," George said, not trying to disguise his anger.

"Nice concept, George. But when you're investigating a murder, nice concepts don't help."

"Come, Jessica," George said. "I think we've lingered long enough."

"Mrs. Fletcher," Josephs said. "Did you know that Kimberly Steffer and Brett Pearl had an affair?"

"No, I did not." Kimberly hadn't confided that in me. Nor had I read anything about it in her diary.

"How do you know this?" I asked.

"That's confidential, too, Mrs. Fletcher."

"Jessica," said George. "Come."

"You're a brave soul, Mrs. Fletcher, to be out walking the bridge again. Even with Scotland Yard at your side."

"Good day, Detective Josephs," I said.

George was openly angry about the conversation that had transpired. "His tone was accusatory. A thoroughly disagreeable man," he said as we walked in the direction of the quaint town of Sausalito. "What cheek!"

I laughed to make light of it. "He's just a type," I said. "Lacking in bedside manner. Interesting what he said about Kimberly having had an affair with her illustrator, Brett Pearl. I wonder if it's true."

"Frankly, I wouldn't believe anything that man says."

*   *   *

The Beat generation lives on; at least that's the impression one gets when strolling the streets of Sausalito. It's charming in a Bohemian way, although the artists and craftsmen who made the town of seven thousand so popular have pretty much abandoned it in favor of a community of houseboats at the north end. But the physical beauty of the town hasn't changed, plummeting down from steep hillsides to the gently curving shoreline.

"Reminds me of the Riviera," George said as we promenaded along the main street.

"I think they call it the Riviera of the West, or something like that," I said. "Feel like coffee?"

"Very much."

We entered the Alta Mira Hotel on Bulkley Street and asked if there was a coffee shop. The young woman's answer was to escort us to a terrace that afforded a spectacular view of the city and bay. She offered us a table. "We're just having coffee," I said. "That's fine," she said.

"Cappuccino, George?"

"Fine."

"Two cappuccinos," I said.

She returned with our coffees, and the day's newspaper. Neither of us would have bothered reading it, not with the view to enjoy. But there was no way to avoid the headline blaring out from the front page.

ARREST IMMINENT IN BRIDGE MURDER.

Just below the headline was a head shot of Brett Pearl. It provided my first glimpse of what he looked like—young, dark, brooding doe-like eyes, soft black curly hair.

Only two paragraphs of the story were on Page One; it jumped to an inside page. I read it aloud for George's benefit.

"An arrest is imminent in the death of Brett Pearl, the man police now say was pushed to his death from the Golden Gate Bridge. This paper has learned that police are holding a former roommate of Pearl's as their prime suspect. Pearl, a noted illustrator of children's books, had been a collaborator with children's author Kimberly Steffer, who was convicted of the murder of her husband, Mark Steffer, three years ago, and is currently incarcerated at the Women's Correctional Facility. Sources further claim that the tip leading to Pearl's former roommate came, in fact, from Ms. Steffer herself."

I handed the paper to George, who continued reading. He gave me a summary as he went.

"The former roommate is a chap named Norman Lana. That's the chap Ms. Steffer mentioned. She said we should talk to him. Let me see. According to this reporter, an anonymous source—Lord, when will the press stop quoting unattributed sources?— this unnamed source says that this Lana fellow and Pearl had a fight the night before Pearl's demise. The fight became violent, and police were called to the scene. Lana was brought in for questioning late last night."

He handed the paper back to me.

"Following the tip, ostensibly from Kimberly Steffer, police went to the restaurant, 'New Dawn,' where Lana had worked as a waiter for the past three months, and he was taken in for questioning. Lana was still being detained at press time, although he had not been formally charged with the murder."

The final paragraphs said: *"In a related incident involving noted mystery writer Jessica Fletcher, police refuse to speculate whether an attempt to push her off the bridge within minutes of the Pearl incident is, in some way, linked to his death."*

"I wonder why Josephs didn't mention this to us a few minutes ago," George said, his face set in a very serious frown.

"I know what I want to do," I said.

"What's that?"

"Meet again with Kimberly Steffer. Excuse me."

I found a phone, called the correctional facility, returned to the table, and said, "Drink up, George. Visiting hours are limited today. It's already eleven. We have to be there by noon."

Kimberly looked exhausted. The harsh overhead lights in the Visitor's Room didn't help. Circles under her eyes had weight to them. She was even paler than usual.

"Kimberly," I said, "the police have taken into custody Brett Pearl's former roommate, Norman

Lana. The press claims that the authorities acted on a tip they received from you."

"That's not true," she said in an almost inaudible voice.

"And we were told this morning by a Detective Josephs that you and Pearl had had an affair."

She laughed sarcastically. "Brett was hardly my type, Mrs. Fletcher. Where did they ever get that idea?"

"I don't know."

"All unsubstantiated gossip," George said, "and without attribution."

"I suppose it doesn't matter," Kimberly said in that same soft, defeated voice.

"It matters to Mrs. Fletcher," said George. "One bloody rumor is that she was out on the Golden Gate the other morning to meet with Brett Pearl. The same morning he fell to his death, and she was almost pushed over."

"I'm sorry to hear that," said Kimberly. "But it isn't my fault. Nothing is my fault. I'm the one sitting behind bars."

"I understand how you feel," I said. "It must be difficult to keep yourself thinking positive, to not give up. Playing the victim won't help, though. Yes, you're behind bars for a crime I'm convinced you didn't commit. But Brett Pearl is dead, and Norman Lana is evidently about to be charged in that murder."

"In other words, Ms. Steffer," George said, "while Mrs. Fletcher is squarely in your corner, you're going to have to keep your chin up and not feel sorry for yourself."

I studied Kimberly's face. George's words had an impact. I wasn't sure if she was going to cry or going to express anger. Quivering lips and glaring eyes can be precursors to either reaction.

Sadness prevailed. "I know," she said to me. "But it isn't easy being here for something you didn't do. I almost think it was better before you came to see me, Mrs. Fletcher. You gave me hope. It was easier when I didn't have any."

"Under that philosophy, you now have double reason to feel that way. Inspector Sutherland believes in your innocence, too."

"I know that, and I'm sincerely grateful to both of you. It's just that—" She swallowed hard and turned her head to hide tears from us.

"It's all right, Kimberly," I said. "I know you're upset. Is there anything else? Are you feeling okay physically?"

"Fighting a cold, that's all," she said. "Sniffles and a sore throat. Nothing compared to when your spirit gets sick."

"Of course," I said. "We came here because I wanted to hear from your mouth that this rumor of an affair between you and Brett Pearl is just that, a rumor without foundation."

"Brett and I never had an affair."

"And to confirm that it wasn't you who informed the police about Norman Lana's possible involvement."

"I did not do that."

"I believe you, Kimberly. We'll be going. But we'll be back soon. In the meantime, Kimberly, don't lose your faith. If you do, I'm liable to lose mine."

George and I took a taxi back to the hotel.

"Well?" I asked as we stood in the lobby, poised to go to our respective rooms.

"I've always believed in her innocence, Jessica. That opinion hasn't changed. But there was something in her demeanor today, almost theatrical, that bothered me."

"I defer to your experience in sizing up accused criminals. Can you be more specific?"

"No. But we have a saying in Scotland. *'There's nocht sae queer as folk.'* "

"Which means?"

"The heart of man, or woman, is more unfathomable than all other natural phenomena. Roughly that."

"Meaning she might have had an affair with Brett Pearl?"

"Of course. I have an old Scottish saying for you, too, my dear Jessica."

"I'm all ears, as we say."

" *'Ye breed o Saughton swine, your neb's never oot o an ill turn.'* "

"Sounds dreadful."

"It can be. It means, loosely, that you are never happy unless you are uprooting something and making trouble."

"You're not the first person to have told me that, George."

"But the first to say it in Scottish."

"Yes. Somehow, it sounds more palatable in a foreign tongue. Bailing out?"

"To the contrary. I'm very much in. You won't get rid of me that easily. What's next, Mrs. Fletcher?"

Chapter Fifteen

"Joan Fontaine," I answered matter-of-factly. "Or Vivien Leigh. Of course, I'd be pleased if Angela Lansbury played me in a film version of my book."

I'd been asked the question by a student in Rhet's public relations class.

"Who are *they*?" a girl asked.

I looked to George, who failed to suppress a smile.

"They're very fine actresses," I replied.

"How about Julia Roberts?" someone asked.

"Or Madonna," another suggested.

"I'm afraid Julia Roberts would be a little too young to play me," I said pleasantly. "And Madonna? I'm not quite sure she would be—well, right for the part. Next question. Yes, young man?" I pointed to a student whose hand was raised. It was refreshing to see hands go up instead of questions being shouted, like in the real world of press conferences.

"Michael McCoy with the *San Francisco Chronicle*, ma'am."

I had to smile. His intense seriousness was adorable. And he was visibly nervous. "Mrs. Fletcher, answer me just this if you will. Mrs. Fletcher, let me ask you—" He fumbled with pages of his notepad and started again. "Ah, yes. Okay. Mrs. Fletcher, will you be involved in the adaptation of your book into a movie script?"

Several other students laughed. In addition to taking himself so seriously, the young man had a stammer, as well as a severe case of acne. I was glad to see the teacher motion for his peers to quiet down.

"That's a very good question, Mr.—McCoy, was it? I'm glad you asked it." He seemed pleased. "Many novelists see their manuscripts fall into the hands of someone else," I said. "Professional screenwriters. When this happens, you run the risk of having your art, your 'masterpiece,' interpreted by someone who doesn't capture the essence of what you've written. On the other hand, some book writers are asked to adapt their own work for the screen. Doing that can be a mixed blessing. The money is nice, of course. And the temptation is always strong to be involved in the process to minimize the risk of a bad adaptation. But, Mr. McCoy, to answer your question, I think I'll stay out of the process of making my book into a motion picture. Screenwriting is not 'my thing,' as you might put it, so I'll leave it to the pros and hope for the best."

"Thank you, Mrs. Fletcher," he said proudly.

"Thank you for asking, Mr. McCoy."

"I think Mrs. Fletcher has time for one more

question," Rhet said. She'd introduced me to open the mock conference, and stood to my right. Her aunt Camille beamed proudly from the last row of the small room. George Sutherland, trooper that he was, sat in the midst of the students, his raincoat tossed casually on a chair next to him, his expression a combination of respect and mirth.

"Yes?" I said, pointing to a tall girl sitting directly behind George.

She stood and said in a clear, firm voice, "I'm Ellie Steffer, with the *San Francisco Examiner*, Mrs. Fletcher. I know you've written many books. Are all of them murder mysteries? Have you ever written about anything else?"

Ellie Steffer!

Having her stand there surprised me so much that her question passed directly through my brain and out my short-term memory. I looked to George, whose wide-open eyes and furrowed brow said clearly that he, too, knew who she was.

"Would you mind repeating the question, Ms. Steffer?" I said.

"Sure." She looked down at a pad of paper and repeated it.

"As a matter of fact, I have written about things other than murder," I said, hoping my voice didn't testify to the shock I still suffered. "Early in my writing career, I wrote two short novels dealing with relationships, at least from the perspective of how a young woman—probably *too* young—viewed them. One was eventually published to resounding silence from readers and critics alike. It was then I turned to writing about murder, which was just beginning to emerge as a popular genre of book. I've never looked back. Does that answer your question?"

"Yes, it does. Thank you."

I desperately wanted to reverse roles, to fire questions at her. Rhet ended the conference, thanked me for being there, and wished me great success with my new book and its film version. She handled herself like Camille, poised and professional. Little doubt she'd be a success one day in whatever field she chose to pursue.

The teacher joined us as the students filed from the room. I looked to where Ellie had sat. She was still there.

Rhet extended her hand. "Mrs. Fletcher, thank you so much. You were wonderful."

"Congratulations to you, Rhet, on a fine job yourself. Your aunt is obviously pleased, and justifiably proud."

"You bet I am," said Camille.

"Certainly worthy of an A," George said to Rhet's teacher.

"I couldn't agree more," replied the teacher.

"I'll walk you out," Rhet said. "I told your driver to be back at eleven-thirty." She checked her Swatch Watch. "Great. Eleven-thirty on the dot."

"Coming, Ms. Steffer?" I asked as we headed for the door.

Ellie continued to sit.

"Come on," Rhet said, waving to her.

Ellie slowly got up and joined us.

"Mrs. Fletcher, this is a friend of mine, Ellie Stef-fer," Rhet said.

"Nice to meet you Ellie," I said. "This is Scotland Yard Inspector George Sutherland."

"Scotland Yard," Rhet said with a chuckle. "Boy, I'm impressed."

I desperately wanted to pull Ellie aside, but knew I couldn't do that. As we progressed toward the lobby, the two girls fell behind, but not so far that I couldn't hear what they were saying. Ellie said to Rhet, "No. Don't."

"Why not?" Rhet said. "She won't mind."

I stopped and said, "What won't I mind?"

"Ellie wants your autograph, Mrs. Fletcher, but she's embarrassed to ask you for it."

"Of course," I said.

Ellie handed me her notepad. As she did, our eyes met. There was an unstated awareness on her part of who I was, and why we shared a special knowledge. Somehow, I had the distinct feeling she wanted to speak with me as much as I wanted to talk to her. It took every ounce of willpower for me not to say something to encourage further conversation. Instead, I dutifully wrote: "To Ellie. Good Luck. Jessica Fletcher."

We continued to the lobby. Through floor-to-ceiling windows I saw the driver holding open one of the car's rear doors. During a final round of good-byes, I decided I would not allow the moment to pass without, at least, making some meaningful contact

with Ellie. But another sight through the windows
stopped me from following through. Ellie's godmother, Nancy Antonio, was seated on a wooden
bench not far from the main door. Without another
word, Ellie stuffed the paper with my autograph into
a pocket of her green school warmup jacket, exited
the school, and went directly to where Nancy Antonio waited. She looked back once. Our eyes locked
through the glass.

"Ready, Jessica?" Camille asked.

"What? Oh, yes, of course. I was daydreaming."

"Perfect day for it," said George, pushing open
the heavy door for me.

"Not quite," I said. His expression said that he
knew exactly what I meant.

We didn't discuss Ellie Steffer's unexpected presence in the class that morning until we'd dropped
Camille off at her office. Once we were alone in the
large rear compartment of the limo, George said, "I
admire your restraint."

"Don't," I said. "I blew a perfect opportunity. I
should have said something. She *wanted* me to say
something. Damn! Why didn't I—?"

"At least you know what she looks like," George
said.

I felt a sneeze brewing. "Kleenex?" I asked.

"I think so." He reached into his raincoat pocket
and pulled out a small traveling pack of tissues—
and a slip of paper. He handed me the tissues just
in time for me to catch the sneeze, and unfolded

the small piece of paper. "Look here, Jessica," he said, handing it to me.

"I need to talk to you, Mrs. Fletcher. But I'm afraid. I'll cut school tomorrow and be at the Mermaid Fountain in Ghirardelli Square at nine. I hope you will be there. Sincerely, Eleanore Steffer."

"She slipped it into my pocket," George said.

"Evidently. Your turn."

"My turn?"

"To walk away from an appearance with something you didn't arrive with. Just like me with Kimberly Steffer's diary. Now a note from her stepdaughter."

"You will go," he said.

"Of course."

"Want me to tag along?"

"Yes. But I don't think you should be with me when I meet with her. Might be inhibiting."

"Be there, but out of sight."

"If you don't mind."

"It's your case, Inspector Fletcher. I'm a good soldier. I follow orders."

"You're the finest kind of pork, George."

"I beg your pardon."

"A sincere compliment in Maine. Nothing to do with pigs. It just means that you are a terrific person."

"Finest kind of pork. People in Maine have a strange way of speaking."

"Almost as strange as a certain Scotsman I know."

I glanced at Ellie's note again. "She says she's afraid. Of what?"

"More important, afraid of *whom*? If we find that out, I believe we'll know who really did kill Mark Steffer."

Chapter Sixteen

"A quick lunch?" I asked George when we reached the hotel.

"Love to, Jessica. But I promised to have lunch today with a colleague from Thailand. Interesting chap. I helped revamp the Thai police department a few years back, and worked closely with him. He attended the conference. Like me, he's extending his stay in San Francisco."

"Another page from the life of George Sutherland I didn't know about. Go enjoy your lunch. Maybe he'll take you to a sushi restaurant."

George laughed. "I've already headed off that possibility by making reservations at Harris's. Excellent steak house I enjoyed my last trip here. Meat and potatoes."

"Sounds yummy. Will I see you later this afternoon?"

"Of course. I intend to do a little shopping after lunch, but should be back by five. Meet in the bar?"

"I'd never turn down a date in the Compass Rose." The bar of that name off the Westin St.

Francis's lobby was the most attractive bar in San Francisco. At least it got my vote. "It's a date," I said.

I went to my room where the message light was blinking furiously. I checked the voice mail system. Eleven calls, most from reporters, who'd obviously figured out that Camille's information about my whereabouts was what's popularly called these days "disinformation." A lie by any other name. The *Chronicle's* crime reporter, Bobby McCormick, who'd followed the Kimberly Steffer case so closely, had left a message. So had Detective Walter Josephs, saying it was urgent that we speak. There were also two calls from Cabot Cove, one from Sheriff Morton Metzger, the other from my good friend, Dr. Seth Hazlitt.

I was tempted to ignore Josephs' call, but there was a urgency in his voice that was compelling. I dialed his number. He picked up on the first ring. "Jessica Fletcher returning your call, Detective."

"Yeah. I was about to give up."

"I wasn't aware I was supposed to be on tap for you," I said coldly.

"No offense, Mrs. Fletcher. Look, I would really appreciate it if you would come down to headquarters right away."

"For what purpose?"

"For the purpose of taking part in a lineup."

"A lineup? For what?"

"To see whether you might recognize somebody who was on the bridge with you that morning."

"I told you I was unaware of people around me."

"Right. Like you told me you hadn't mentioned to anyone that you were planning to take that walk across the bridge. I can't make you come down, but I think you should."

I thought for a moment before saying, "All right. Does it have to do with the arrest of Norman Lana?"

"You read about that, huh?"

"Yes. I was surprised you didn't mention it to us when we met on the other side of the bridge yesterday."

"It slipped my mind. Can you be here in an hour?"

"Could we make it an hour and a half? I haven't had lunch, and I'm famished."

"Sure. See you then. By the way, you can put in for cab fare."

"I wasn't thinking about expenses, Detective. Good-bye."

Despite my growling stomach, I returned the calls to Mort and Seth in Cabot Cove. I didn't reach Mort; his desk sergeant informed me that the sheriff was out investigating the reported theft of someone's chicken. But I got through to Seth, who'd just returned from tending to a patient at our local hospital. "Gorry, it's good to hear your voice, Jessica," he said. Seth had the heaviest Maine accent of anyone I've ever known. I sometimes wondered if he worked at thickening it for effect.

"Nice to hear your voice, too," I said.

"Are you all right?"

I laughed. "Of course I'm all right. Don't believe everything you read."

"I thought you were comin' back after your tour."

"I am. But I decided to extend my time here for a well-deserved vacation. George and I have been—"

"George and you? That Detective Sutherland fella?"

"Yes. He was here at a police conference—"

"I know, Jessica. He decided to extend his stay there, too, for a well-deserved vacation."

He sounded angry.

"Jessica, if you're plannin' to be there through the upcomin' weekend, I just might see you in San Francisco."

"Really? Why?"

"Got an invitation to attend a medical seminar on hypnosis. You know how much I enjoy that subject."

Seth Hazlitt, despite how old-fashioned he could be both personally and medically—he always referred to himself as a "chicken soup doctor"—also had a fascination with less mainstream medical disciplines, like the use of hypnosis as a therapeutic tool. He'd attended seminars on the subject taught by the world's leading authorities, including two conducted by Dr. Herbert Spiegel at New York's Columbia University's College of Physicians and Surgeons. I have always admired Seth for being openminded enough to embrace new, sometimes controversial approaches to medicine.

"That would be—lovely," I said, hoping my voice did not mirror my disappointment in hearing that he might join me in San Francisco. Not that I didn't love Seth dearly. But I'd been so busy, and desperately wanted some quiet, relaxing time with George. Having Seth arrive would only complicate what was already too complicated a life.

"Haven't made up my mind yet whether to come or not, Jess. Have to arrange for coverage. Got three patients in the hospital right now. Have to make sure Doc Simmons can cover for me."

"Of course," I said. "You mustn't run off on your hospitalized patients, Seth. You'd be thinking about them every minute you're here."

"Ayuh. Probably can't break away. What are you and this Sutherland fella up to out there?"

"We're not 'up to' anything. Just enjoying some pleasant dinners. Frankly, he's being a tremendous help in this case I'm following."

"There you go again, Jessica. Doesn't sound like much of a vacation if you're trying to solve another murder."

I lightened my voice. "I'm not trying to solve anything, Seth. Just looking for a few answers to some questions that I never intended to ask. I have to run. I'm starved, and I have an appointment at—"

"An appointment where?"

"At—the hairdresser. Sweet of you to call. How's the weather back there?"

"Cooled off considerably. Much improved."

"Glad to hear that."

"What's the weather out there in San Francisco?"

"Ah, rainy and cold." I realized my lie could be

quickly discovered by flipping on the national weather channel. "Don't believe what you see on TV, Seth. You know how weathermen always get it wrong."

"Ayuh, I certainly know that. You keep in touch, now, heah?"

I promised to do that.

I tried Bobby McCormick at the paper but he was out. I left my name and said I would not be available until late in the afternoon. I headed downstairs where I satisfied my hunger with a crabmeat salad and, of course, the city's honest-to-God sourdough bread. I hailed a cab and headed for police headquarters. Detective Walter Josephs was waiting for me. "Thanks for coming, Mrs. Fletcher," he said. "Please follow me."

He led me to a dark, claustrophobic room. A large two-way mirrored window afforded a view of the adjoining room, where five men stood in front of a wall on which a height chart had been crudely painted. They all seemed to be staring at me, although I knew they couldn't see because of the special properties of the glass separating us.

A microphone in the other room picked up their shuffling, and occasional sneeze or cough. They all looked somewhat alike, which, I knew, was done deliberately when mounting a lineup. One would be the suspect; the others would be drawn from different walks of life, including from the ranks of the police itself. Each man had a full head of black, curly hair. Their clothing ranged from a business suit on the one to the far right, to scruffy jeans, T-shirt, and torn leather jacket on the man at the left.

"Ready, Mrs. Fletcher?" Josephs asked.

"I suppose so. You want me to determine whether I saw one of these five men on the bridge the morning I was almost pushed off?"

"That's right." Josephs spoke into a microphone: "Okay, okay, shape up in there. Stand at attention and look straight ahead."

I moved closer to the glass, narrowed my eyes and focused on each face. None was even vaguely familiar to me. The only immediate reaction I had was that the young man on the left, who was dressed shabbily, had an unusual face. His features were fine, actually delicate. A feminine face. I thought of the photograph of Brett Pearl that had appeared in the newspaper. They looked somewhat alike, at least according to my recollection of that picture.

"Well?" Josephs asked.

I shook my head and stepped back. "I don't recognize any of them."

"Certain about that?"

"Yes."

Josephs spoke into the microphone again: "Turn around. slow. Left profile to the glass."

I returned to my position up close to the window and took in their left profiles. Then I was treated to a look at the right side of their faces. Finally, Josephs had them stand with their backs to me.

"I'm sorry, Detective Josephs, but none of them

are known to me. As I told you, I wasn't aware of other people on the bridge, except in a general sense. I wish I could be helpful, but I'm afraid I can't be in this instance."

"Nothing ventured, nothing gained," he mumbled. "My old man liked to say that."

I smiled. "Mind if I ask which of the five men in that room is your suspect?"

"Suspect? Who said we had a suspect in there?"

"No one said it, but I assume one of them is Norman Lana."

He broke into a crooked grin. "Can't put anything over on you, huh, Mrs. Fletcher? Yeah. Lana is the one on the left."

The one with the delicate, feminine features.

"Has he been charged in Brett Pearl's murder?" I asked.

Josephs shook his head. "We've held him as a potential suspect, but we don't have enough to keep him any longer. He'll float out of here, back to the Castro with the rest of them."

My face reflected my puzzlement. "Back to 'the Castro'? What's that?"

"The Castro. Our famous gay community. You have heard we have a few homosexuals out here in San Francisco."

"Yes, of course."

"Well, Lana is pretty well known in the Castro. Works as a waiter these days in town, but does an occasional stint as a female impersonator."

"Interesting," I said.

"If you go for that sort of thing."

"Since you can't formally charge Mr. Lana with having pushed Brett Pearl off the bridge, I assume you can't make any charges regarding my near disaster."

"Right."

"But you do think that Mr. Lana might have been the one who attempted to push me off."

"Right again, Mrs. Fletcher. We'll keep on him. Make his life miserable. Sometimes these types crack under that sort of pressure."

I thought of Norman Lana's constitutional rights, but didn't express that to the detective as I followed him back to his office.

"So, have you gotten back to my manuscript?" he asked.

"No, I'm ashamed to say. But I certainly intend to. Tell you what, Detective. You give me a couple of hours with the Kimberly Steffer files right now, and I'll read your manuscript with special care and interest this evening."

Josephs looked as though he was involved in a painful internal struggle. Finally, after much grimacing, he said, "Okay. But unofficial. Same rules as before. Somebody comes in, you say you're doing work for me as a temp."

"Fair enough."

I wondered, of course, whether my now-familiar face in San Francisco would render that lie absurd, but decided not to worry about it. That was his problem.

My two hours in front of the computer yielded little information. I did find various photographs of Kimberly Steffer, obtained during the course of the investigation and scanned into the police computer system, to be of interest. She was a strikingly beautiful young woman, with a vitality and freshness to her face. She'd worn her lovely blond hair in various styles. Some pictures had her wearing it long, beyond shoulder-length. In others, she'd had it cut severely short. But she was one of those women for whom it didn't matter how she wore her hair. She was stunning in an understated sense no matter what style she chose.

When I was finished, I told Josephs I was returning to the hotel. This time he didn't offer a ride. But he did remind me once again of my promise to go over his dreadful manuscript that evening. The thought of it was as appealing as facing a firing squad, but I pledged to myself to uphold my end of the bargain. I said I would call him in the morning with my evaluation, and left the building where a taxi stood waiting for a fare.

My driver was a heavyset Hispanic gentleman. He wore a baseball cap with the emblem of the San Francisco Giants on it. Sunlight coming through the window highlighted deep acne scarring on his full cheeks. His glasses had strikingly thick lenses.

I leaned forward to read the hack license affixed to the glove compartment. Phillipe Fernandez.

Why was that name familiar? I grappled with the question for a minute. Then, it hit me. That was the name of the cabdriver who'd testified at Kimberly Steffer's trial that he'd picked her up at the mall the day of Mark Steffer's murder. Much had been made of his poor eyesight, which evidently hadn't played much of a role in the jury's deliberations and ultimate verdict.

I attempted to engage him in conversation, but he didn't seem particularly interested in small talk. He dropped me at the hotel. I paid the fare and lingered for a moment to take in his face. He didn't look like a man that would lie to hurt another person, but I knew that was a silly conclusion to come to based upon a brief physical examination. I stepped back and thanked him for a pleasant ride. He didn't respond, simply drove away.

The cab company for which he drove was the Express Cab Company. A half hour later, after showering and changing into fresh clothing, I looked up the phone number for the company and called it.

"Express Cab Company," a man said with an accent I judged to be Hispanic.

"Yes, hello. I was in one of your cabs earlier this afternoon. I was picked up in front of police headquarters and driven to the Westin St. Francis Hotel. My driver's name was Phillipe Fernandez."

"Yes?" the man said. "You have a problem?"

"Yes, I do, as a matter of fact. I had a small black bag with me that I left in Mr. Fernandez's taxi. I was wondering—"

"Hold on. He's here. He just got off duty."

Phillipe Fernandez came on the phone. I repeated my story to him. "Did you find it by any chance?" I asked.

"No."

"Gee, I'm sorry to hear that," I said. "Do you remember me? You picked me up at police headquarters."

"Sure, the blond lady. Red blazer."

"That's me," I said. "You have a good memory." I didn't add that his eyesight was better than it appeared to be.

"No bag. I find no bag."

"Well, maybe I'm mistaken and left it some other place."

"You give me your number in case I find it."

"No, but thank you. I'll call back tomorrow to see if it turned up."

"Okay." The sound of the phone being hung up clicked in my ear.

It was almost five. I wondered if George had returned from his lunch and shopping expedition. I dialed his room but received his voice mail: "Jessica here, George. I'm in my room. Give a call when you come in."

I pulled Detective Josephs' partially completed manuscript from a dresser drawer and settled in to begin the unpleasant chore of reading it once again, this time with an eye toward making editorial notes that would at least indicate I'd tried. But I hadn't gotten through the first page when the phone rang.

I assumed it was George, picked it up, and said, "Hi. How was your lunch?"

There was silence on the other end. "George?"

"No. Is this Jessica Fletcher?"

"Yes, it is." My heart sunk. Obviously a reporter. That left me with the choice of rudely hanging up, or answering questions.

But then I was made aware that this was not a reporter calling me.

"Mrs. Fletcher, my name is Norman Lana."

Chapter Seventeen

"George, I had to run out for a few hours. It's now five. I hope to be back here at the hotel by seven. I'll call you then. But please don't wait for me if you can make other plans for dinner. Leave a message on my voice mail and maybe we'll catch up somewhere tonight."

That message left, I took a few minutes to read my San Francisco guidebook about the section of the city known as the Castro, named after Castro Street that runs through the heart of it. It is, as the book pointed out, one of the largest concentrations of homosexuals in America. The book also made the point that a tremendous program of gentrification had taken place, turning that area into a vital, vibrant part of the greater San Francisco area, as well as a popular tourist destination.

I gave the cabdriver Norman Lana's address and settled back. Lana had suggested we meet in a bar around the corner from where he lived, but I was uncomfortable with that. He sounded as though he had something important to tell me; it's been my experience that public places, especially noisy bars, are seldom the right venue for exchanging meaningful information.

The guidebook was right. As we proceeded down Castro Street, I took in the hustle bustle going on all along the avenue. Although it was still daylight, the area had the festive feeling of much later at night, when bars and restaurants would be going full tilt.

We turned off Castro and stopped in front of a pretty, narrow three-story building painted in a pastel apricot tint, with contrasting blue paint on its shutters and front door. I paid the driver, and stood on the sidewalk. Lana said he lived on the top floor, which was confirmed by his name next to the uppermost buzzer in a vertical row of three. One apartment to a floor, I gathered as I pushed the button.

His voice came through a tiny speaker. "Mrs. Fletcher?" I confirmed that it was. "Come on up." A buzzer sounded, releasing the latch on the inside door.

Lana stood at the top of the two flights of stairs. He was dressed as he had been at the lineup at police headquarters. His smile was wide and engaging. I shook his extended hand. "Come in, please, Mrs. Fletcher. It was good of you to come so quickly."

The apartment was neat as a pin, and tastefully decorated and furnished. The walls of the large living room were a delicate yellow, the oversize trim painted a brilliant white. A large, obviously expensive Oriental rug covered most of the wood floor, whose exposed edges were burnished to a high luster. Tasteful paintings and prints were everywhere.

"What a pretty place," I said.

"Thank you. Where I live means a lot to me. I need order and cleanliness."

"So do I," I said.

"Something to drink? Wine? I have a nice selection."

"No, thank you."

"Tea? Coffee?"

"A cup of tea would be lovely," I said, sitting in a small green armchair by the window.

Lana returned a minute later from the kitchen with a steaming mug of tea on a small silver tray. A bowl of sugar, and a delicate Japanese pitcher held what turned out to be half-and-half. He pulled a leather director's chair from a corner and sat across a glass table from me. He'd opted for a glass of white wine, which he raised in a toast. "To having the pleasure of sitting with America's foremost mystery writer," he said.

I lifted my teacup and said, "It's a pleasure meeting you, Mr. Lana, although I'm not sure the rest of what you said is worthy of a toast."

"Ever been to the Castro?" he asked.

"No. I've been to San Francisco many times, but never had the pleasure of seeing this part of town."

Lana laughed. "No, I suppose you wouldn't. Unless, of course, you had a friend here."

"Exactly. You said you wanted to talk to me about something very important, Mr. Lana. What is that?"

He sat back in his chair and fixed his gaze on the wineglass he held in both hands. Finally, he placed the glass on the table, leaned forward, and said, "I don't know whether you're aware of it, Mrs. Fletcher, but I've been accused of pushing Brett Pearl off the Golden Gate Bridge."

"Yes, I am aware of that. I read the newspapers."

He shook his head. "No, you know it for reasons other than what the newspapers have written. You were at police headquarters today when they put me in a lineup."

I chewed my cheek and thought of a response. How would he know that? I did the logical thing. I asked.

"I saw you leave the building," he said. "They held me for a while after the lineup, then said I could go, not because they decided I didn't push Brett off the bridge, but because they don't have enough evidence to hold me beyond a certain point. I'm not a lawyer, but I do know that much."

I nodded and sipped my tea.

"They also questioned me about whether I had anything to do with the accident you had on the bridge."

I raised my eyebrows and smiled. "I would hardly call it an accident. Someone *did* try to push me off."

"Bad choice of words," he said. "More tea?"

"No. Did you—did *you* try to push me off the bridge?"

My directness shocked him into silence. He recovered, gave forth his infectious grin, and replied, "I certainly did not, Mrs. Fletcher. If there's anything you can believe about what's been going on, believe that."

I didn't commit myself to a response, and waited for him to continue.

"I suppose I sound as though I'm talking around the reason I wanted to speak with you. I had a conversation with Kimberly after I left police headquarters."

"You did? How did that come about?"

"I called her."

"And they allowed you to speak with her?"

"Yes. I called because I need someone to stand up for me, to verify what I'm about to tell you." He scrutinized me for a reaction, but didn't get one. I was determined to offer as little as possible, but to take in as much as he was willing to offer.

"Kimberly is one of the few people in this world who knows the real situation between Brett and me. I suppose you read we were roommates."

"Yes."

"We were, but not for very long. You see, Mrs. Fletcher, the problem is—" He sat back again and closed his eyes tight. I wondered if he was about to cry. When he opened his eyes, they were moist. "Brett and I were lovers."

I suppose my expression reflected my surprise at that statement, although what he'd just said hadn't come from left field. After having read that they were roommates, and factoring in Detective Josephs' comment about Lana's sexual orientation, I wondered whether they had, in fact, been lovers.

Lana continued to reinforce that possibility. "The difficulty was, Mrs. Fletcher, that I've been out of the closet, as they say, for a long time. But Brett never acknowledged his homosexuality. He kept it a big, dark secret from everyone except a select few friends. Kimberly was one of those friends."

I silently questioned his use of the term "friends." From what I'd learned, Kimberly Steffer and Brett Pearl were hardly that. Pearl had sued her. According to Kimberly, it had been a nasty episode in her life, and her husband, Mark, had had confrontations with Pearl about the lawsuit.

All I said to the young man across the table from me was, "Go on. I'm listening."

"Even though we stopped living together, we continued our relationship right up until Brett jumped to his death."

It came involuntarily from me. "Jumped?"

Lana enthusiastically nodded and slid to the edge of his chair. "That's exactly what happened, Mrs. Fletcher. For some reason, the police have decided that Brett was pushed to his death, murdered. Some witness supposedly saw it happen. But that isn't true. It's a damn lie. Brett jumped—killed himself— because we'd ended our relationship the day before."

I said, "I know jilted lovers sometimes take the drastic step of ending their lives, but it's hard for me to accept the reality of anyone doing that over a broken relationship of the sort you and he had."

I wondered if he was thinking the same thing as I was, that I'd just demonstrated classic homophobia in discounting the depth of feelings that could develop between two men, or two women. I certainly didn't mean that.

If Lana was thinking the same thing, he didn't indicate it. He said, "I know it's hard to believe. But that's why I called Kimberly. Brett had once told her that if anything ever happened to end our relationship, he would kill himself. I called hoping that Kimberly would remember that conversation."

"And? Did she?"

"Yes."

I felt the need to get up and stretch my legs. I looked out the window onto the quiet, pretty street, then slowly walked the perimeter of the room, admiring the art on the walls. I could feel Lana's eyes following me. I turned and said, "I don't know whether you know it or not, Mr. Lana, but Kimberly Steffer and I have had a number of face-to-face conversations. I happen to believe in her innocence, and have been spending time here in San Francisco attempting to prove that she did not kill her husband. I will, of course, ask her whether she remembers such a comment from Brett Pearl."

He joined me where I stood by a high-curved archway leading to the bedroom. "I hope you do, Mrs. Fletcher," he said.

We were very close to each other, no more than a

few feet separating us. I'd noticed during the police lineup his feminine features. Now, being in such close proximity, I was struck even harder by that observation. With longer hair, and appropriately dressed, he could pass for a woman. His skin was smooth and flawless, no hint of a beard line. Detective Josephs said that Lana had once made a living as a female impersonator.

"I was told by someone that you had worked as a female impersonator, Mr. Lana."

If I thought the question might make him nervous, I was wrong. He immediately said, "For a couple of years, as a matter of fact. I loved it. I was good at it."

"Is there much work for female impersonators?" I asked.

He laughed softly. "There is here in San Francisco. I worked at Finocchio's. Have you been there?"

"No, I haven't. But I've heard about it. You must have been very good to work there. I understand it's the best club of its kind."

"It sure is. I'd still be there, except they like to change performers on a regular basis. Actually, I had a pretty long run at Finocchio's. If you'd like to go there some night, I can arrange VIP treatment for you."

"That's very kind of you," I said, crossing the room, picking up my cup, and draining the last of the tea. "I may take you up on that."

I took my handbag from the floor and came to

the center of the room. "I really must be going, Mr. Lana. I have to admit that I'm having trouble accepting that Brett Pearl jumped from the bridge, rather than having been pushed. But I'll take your word for it. By the way, how do you know for sure he jumped? He really might have been pushed. After all, having made a comment to Kimberly Steffer a long time ago that he would kill himself hardly stands as evidence that that's what he actually did."

"No, Mrs. Fletcher. I *know* he jumped because I saw him."

"You were on the bridge when he jumped?"

He trained his eyes on the Oriental rug and said softly, "Yes, I was. We'd been arguing for almost twenty-four hours. It had more to do with his refusal to acknowledge his homosexuality than it did with our breakup. We both knew that the relationship was going to end. It had been going downhill for quite a while. I loved him very much, and couldn't stand his refusal to acknowledge who and what he was. I pleaded with him to come out into the daylight. Living that kind of lie is a horrible burden for anyone, Mrs. Fletcher. I know. I lived it for too long myself. The most liberating, joyous day of my life was when I decided to no longer live the lie.

"But I couldn't get Brett to see that. He was petrified at the thought of people knowing he was a gay man. He comes from a very religious family. Nice people. Well-meaning. I got to know his mother and father quite well when we would visit them in England. As far as Brett was concerned, acknowledging to them that he was gay would kill them. He was wrong, of course. People get upset when they hear that a son or daughter is not the person they thought, but most get over it, even end up embracing that same son or daughter. But Brett couldn't deal with it."

"Are you saying that he jumped because of the pain he suffered through grappling with whether to come out of the closet?"

"No. I guess I have to take a lot more blame than I'm comfortable with. The fact is, I threatened that morning to call his mother and father and tell them."

"Why would you do that to someone you loved?"

He shrugged. "I don't know. The heat of an argument is as good a reason as any. I should have tried to dissuade Brett from taking that walk across the bridge. He was beside himself after I'd threatened to expose him to the world. He said he needed to walk, to clear his head. I went with him. When he started across, I had a moment when I questioned whether this was a wise thing for him to be doing. You know the reputation of the Golden Gate Bridge as a suicide site. But we just kept arguing and talking, and walking. When we got to the middle, he stopped and started to cry. I went to put my arms around him, but he slipped away and was gone."

Which meant, of course, that Norman Lana was on the bridge when *I* was almost pushed to my death. Did I need to say that to him?

Evidently not, because the next thing he said was, "And I didn't try to push you, Mrs. Fletcher. Sure, I was on the bridge. I understand your incident took place about the same time as when Brett jumped. I can't change that. All I can do is ask that you believe me."

I didn't know whether I believed him or not, but debating the point wouldn't shed any greater light at that moment. I said, "Thank you for being so open with me, Mr. Lana."

"Please, call me Norman."

"All right, Norman. You've been very forthcoming. You know how to reach me. I'll be in San Francisco for a few more days if you think of anything else you'd like to unburden."

"I appreciate that, Mrs. Fletcher. And please, talk to Kimberly. She'll confirm what I've said."

As I headed for the door, he said, "Would you like to see the rest of the apartment?"

I followed him through the archway to the bedroom, dominated by a king-size bed. The entire wall behind it formed a headboard of shelves filled with books and what I judged to be expensive small artifacts and pieces of sculpture. The walls were cream-colored; the floor was covered by thick burgundy carpeting. As in the living room, a great deal of art hung on the walls.

"It's beautiful, Mr. Lana. Norman. You have a wonderful touch. Have you worked professionally as a decorator?"

"Just helping out friends now and then."

I was about to leave when my eye went to an open closet door. Inside was a life-size mannequin dressed in a heavily sequined dressing gown. The face was that of a woman. A blond wig fell gracefully to the mannequin's shoulders.

Lana noticed my interest in it. He said, laughing, "Just something from my previous life, Mrs. Fletcher. At Finocchio's." He quickly closed the closet door and led me back into the living room.

"Again, thank you for coming," he said.

"I'm glad I did, Norman. Perhaps we'll have a chance to talk again."

Chapter Eighteen

"*Jessica. George here. I got your message and intended to wait at the hotel for you to return. But something has come up that I must attend to, so hope to touch base later. I should be back by ten. If it's later than that, I won't call knowing you're bound to be exhausted and asleep. In that event, we'll ring each other in the morning.*" There was a pause as though he pondered what to say next. "*Take care, dear lady. This will be one very unhappy Scotsman if anything should happen to a dear friend named Jessica Fletcher.*"

I was, at once, disappointed in receiving that message and filled with curiosity. What could have come up that demanded his immediate attention? Silly of me, to say nothing of unfair, to be so questioning of his activities. After all, we didn't owe each other explanations of how we spent our time. Besides, I'd scooted off and hadn't bothered to explain where I was going, or why.

Did the possibility cross my mind that there might be a woman in George's life? Of course it did. It wasn't a serious consideration, but I did wonder about it as I poured myself a mineral water from the suite's bar, kicked off my shoes, and turned on the television. The newscast was dominated by the sort of news we've become accustomed to these days, and shouldn't be—murder, rapes, politicians charged with fraud, natural disasters, man-made disasters, and other items of interest that cause us to shake our heads in disbelief and despair.

As I watched, I pondered what to do with the rest of my evening. It didn't take long for the answer to be provided. I picked up the ringing telephone and heard a familiar voice from the past. "Jessica? This is Neil Schwartz."

"Neil! How wonderful to hear your voice. Where are you calling from? Wisconsin?"

"This cheapskate calling long-distance?" His laugh was guttural and pleasantly recognizable. "I'm calling from right here in San Francisco. Want me to sing a chorus or two?" He began crooning the words to "I Left My Heart in San Francisco." He was so off-key it caused me to giggle.

"Enough," I said. "It's a good thing you decided to make your living as a writer. I'm afraid a career on the stage is not in your future."

"You know how to hurt a man, Jess. No, I'm right here in the same city you are. Took a little tracking down, but perseverance prevailed. Any chance of us grabbing dinner tonight?"

"A very good chance. I happen to be free."

"Wonderful. There will be three of us."

"Oh? Who's the third person?"

"My wife."

"Neil, that's splendid news. When did you get married?"

"Last week. Back home in Madison."

"I thought you were living in Milwaukee."

"I was, but then I got lucky, to say nothing of legitimate, and took an adjunct professor position at the University of Wisconsin. Teaching budding poets why they should consider another career. Jill and I are here on our honeymoon. Met her at the university. She teaches theater."

"I can't wait to meet her," I said.

"An hour?"

"Perfect."

"Someone recommended a terrific sushi place to me here in San Francisco. Restaurant Isuzu."

I didn't hesitate. "Neil, you know I'm generally a very easy person when it comes to picking restaurants. I like just about everything. But since being in San Francisco, I've satisfied my urge for sushi for the next couple of years. Something else? Meat and potatoes?"

"Hold on a second, Jess. Let me consult my list of recommendations. Okay. How about chicken or fish cooked over a wood fire? And mashed potatoes."

"Sounds great," I said.

He said we were going to a "hip" new place called LuLu, on Folsom Street, and that he and his bride would pick me up at the hotel in an hour.

Neil's call, and our dinner date, lifted my spirits.

I showered, dressed in the most elegant evening attire I'd brought with me—certainly at least elegant for this non-fashion plate, whose taste runs more to sweatsuits and cardigan sweaters—and was waiting downstairs when they arrived.

Although Neil Schwartz had thickened in the midsection, and had lost some hair, his simpatico personality hadn't changed. Jill was a shade taller than Neil. Her hair was the color of strawberries, and hundreds of freckles on her broad face created a map of sorts.

We all got along famously, lingering into the night at the cavernous restaurant whose food lived up to Neil's advance billing.

Over snifters of cognac, I said, "There is a certain irony in us getting together here in San Francisco."

He knew what I was getting at because he said, "The Kimberly Steffer case."

"Exactly. I suppose you've learned something of my involvement with it."

"Can't miss it if you read the papers, and watch television. What was this business of you almost being pushed off the Golden Gate Bridge?"

I sighed. "A frightening experience, although it could have been worse had my attacker been successful. I tend to forget about it until someone brings it up."

"Maybe Neil shouldn't have," said Jill.

"No, no, I didn't mean that. I read the chapter in your book, Neil, about Kimberly Steffer. As I recall, you didn't take any sides concerning her guilt or innocence."

"That's right. A lot of people didn't think she did it. But I went with the trial, and the guilty verdict that came out of it. Have you joined the Kimberly Steffer Believer's Club?"

I nodded. "I've spoken with her a few times in prison. I do not believe she murdered her husband." I held up my hands against the next obvious question. "I don't have anything to base that on, Neil. No hard facts. But when you've spent your professional life dealing with murder—most of it fictitious, I acknowledge, but too often real—you develop a sense. By the way, a friend of mine, George Sutherland, is in San Francisco. He's with Scotland Yard in London."

"You mentioned him to me in a letter awhile back."

"I suppose I did. A dear, dear man. I've managed to drag him into the Kimberly Steffer mess, and he seems to share my belief that she's innocent. You wrote about her illustrator, Brett Pearl, in your book."

"Yeah."

"Do you know he fell to his death from the Golden Gate at about the same time someone tried to push me over?"

Both Neil and Jill sat up straighter.

"My God," said Jill. "Did the same person who tried to kill you push *him* over?"

"I would say that's a reasonable assumption," I responded. "The question is, who is that person?"

The subject changed to something more pleasant. As we chatted enthusiastically, I glanced at my watch. Almost eleven. "Would you excuse me while I make a phone call?" I said.

I dialed the Westin St. Francis from a pay phone and asked for George Sutherland's room. I reached his voice mail. "George, this is Jessica. I'm at a delightful dinner with old friends. Well, at least one of them is an old friend, Neil Schwartz. He's here on his honeymoon. He, his wife and I have been celebrating a bit. I hope you're all right. If I get back to the hotel by midnight, I'll give you a call. If not, we'll do as you suggested and meet up in the morning. Sleep tight. And don't worry about me. I'm in good company."

As it turned out, Neil and Jill dropped me at the hotel a few minutes past midnight. I checked my voice mail the moment I got to my suite. The message from George said: *"I checked for messages a bit ago, Jessica, and received yours. Glad you're having a splendid evening with friends. My evening has developed into a rather interesting one, the details of which I will relay to you when we gather forces in the morning. Breakfast at seven? Don't forget you are to meet the young Ms. Steffer at nine. Sleep tight yourself."*

I must admit I was worried about George, but I was also fatigued. After a few minutes of television, I climbed happily into bed and was asleep, it seemed, the moment my head touched my pillow.

Chapter Nineteen

Scotland Yard Inspector George Sutherland is what you might call an even-tempered human being. Few highs, and even fewer lows in mood and behavior. Calm and rational, levelheaded, and very much in control of his emotions.

Which is why I was somewhat taken aback when I met him the following morning in the lobby of our hotel. There was a distinct bounce to his step. His greeting of me was unusually expansive. "Ah, good morning my dear lady," he said beaming. "Have you looked outside? What a magnificent fat day."

"Yes. It looks like we're in for a spell of nice weather. Are we having breakfast here in the hotel?"

"Absolutely not," he said, his tone still a few levels above what it generally is. "I always like to sample the best a city has to offer. I thought breakfast at the Buena Vista was very much in order this morning. I understand its breakfast offerings are unparalleled. Besides, it is close to Ghirardelli Square, where you are to meet with the mysterious Ms. Steffer."

I couldn't help but smile at his ebullient mood.

He'd obviously had an enjoyable evening, and had slept soundly after it. "All right," I said. "Breakfast at the Buena Vista it is."

We exited our taxi and stepped into the famous saloon, where Irish coffee had been introduced to America. The place was jammed even at that early hour. The large, round tables were communal; we waited until two chairs opened up at one, joining six other diners. We placed our breakfast orders—pancakes, two eggs over-easy, and bacon for George; scrambled eggs, dry, and toast for me.

The food was delicious. So was the conversation with our tablemates, two of whom were British on a stopover in San Francisco en route to Hong Kong.

I tried to get George on the subject of the previous evening, but was unsuccessful. He simply continued the conversation with others at the table. Finally, when I asked him again, he said, "In all due course, Jessica. That was a delicious breakfast. I think we'd better head for your nine o'clock appointment."

We walked the short distance from the Buena Vista to Ghirardelli Square and found the Mermaid Fountain in the central plaza. We were a half hour early for my rendezvous with Ellie Steffer. We bought two cappuccinos to go from a nearby coffee shop—there seemed to be coffee shops everywhere—and took them to an empty wrought-iron table in the central plaza. "This is as good a place as any for me to wait for her, I suppose," I said.

"Yes," George agreed. "Quite centrally located,

with a view of the entire area. I suppose I should make myself scarce." He looked across the plaza to another group of tables partially obscured from our view. He laughed. "I feel very much like a house detective in a seedy hotel, hiding behind a potted palm in search of unsavory goings-on."

"You can stay right here with me if you wish."

"No. As we agreed, my presence might inhibit the young lady from being candid. She obviously has something very important on her mind, and it seems you are about to become the recipient of whatever that is. I'll be over there."

He started to walk away.

"George," I said.

He stopped and turned. "Yes, Jessica?"

"Where were you last night?"

His smile was again expansive. "As my dear, departed father said, patience is truly a virtue. This afternoon."

"I have to wait until this afternoon to find out what you did last night? To find out why you're in such wonderful spirits this morning?"

"Exactly. I'll be right over there in case you need me." With that, he took purposeful strides in the direction of his secluded vantage point.

I sat at the table and sipped my cappuccino. George's festive demeanor had kept my mind from dwelling upon the meeting I was about to have with Ellie Steffer. But now as I sat alone, I was bombarded with a series of thoughts and concerns.

What if, instead of Ellie, her mother, Joan, or

godmother, Nancy Antonio, showed up? My one run-in with Ms. Antonio had been enough to last me a lifetime. It was possible that either woman might keep Ellie's appointment for her. Nancy Antonio had been sitting right outside the school when Ellie left. Then again, she might not have known of my appearance. I decided to go on the assumption that she did know, and be on the lookout for her.

And what of Ellie's mother? I'd yet to meet her. But maybe Ellie had told *her* that I'd been at her school for my mock press conference.

As these, and other thoughts came to me, I decided it was a fruitless exercise to worry about things that were not, at least as yet, reality. I would find out soon enough what the morning held for me.

Provided, of course, that Ellie or *someone* showed up. I was thinking of the possibility that no one would arrive at Ghirardelli Square when I looked across the plaza and saw Ellie standing at its perimeter. She surveyed the area, looking for me, I assumed. And then I saw Camille's niece, Rhet, come to Ellie's side. Interesting, I thought. I knew they were friends from their interplay at school. But why would Rhet accompany her to meet with me? That would mean, I surmised, that she knew what was going on.

I was tempted to stand and wave, but didn't. I didn't want to draw attention to myself, or to the fact that we were meeting. I didn't have to. Rhet spotted me, said something to Ellie, and the girls approached.

"Hello, Rhet," I said. "Hello, Ellie."

"Hi, Mrs. Fletcher," Rhet said enthusiastically. Ellie averted my eyes, focusing her attention on some unseen point in the distance.

"Join me?" I asked. "I have coffee from that shop over there. Can I get you girls something?"

"No, thank you, Mrs. Fletcher," Rhet said. She turned to Ellie, who had turned deadly serious. "Ellie, come on, this was your idea."

I sat silently and waited for Ellie to make a decision whether to sit or to bolt. Eventually, she took a chair next to Rhet.

"Do they have lemonade?" Ellie asked, looking in the direction of the coffee shop.

"I would imagine," I said. I pulled a five-dollar bill from my purse and placed it on the table. "My treat. But hurry back."

Instead of both girls leaving the table, it was Ellie who walked away carrying the money. When she was out of earshot, Rhet leaned closer and said, "She's really scared to be talking to you, Mrs. Fletcher."

"Why, for heaven's sake?"

"Because—well, because if her mother or her godmother knew she was here, she'd be in big trouble. I mean b-i-g trouble."

"And I certainly wouldn't want to be the cause of that," I said. "Rhet, did either Ellie's mother, or Ms. Antonio, know that I made a presentation at your school?"

"Oh, boy, no. If they knew Ellie had come to

school that day to hear you talk, they would have been furious."

"What a difficult way for a young girl to live," I said, shaking my head. "I feel sorry for her."

"So do I. That's why I came with her today."

"You're obviously a good friend."

"I like Ellie. I wouldn't say we're real close, but I enjoy being with her. She's very smart. I just wish she wasn't so sad."

"Having your father murdered must leave a terrible mark on you," I said.

"Especially when the person who did it isn't in jail, and the one who didn't do it is—in jail, I mean."

"You're talking about Kimberly Steffer."

"Yes. Kimberly Steffer was not—"

Rhet stopped speaking as Ellie returned to the table carrying two plastic cups of lemonade. She resumed her chair and took a cigarette from the pocket of her black leather jacket. "Do you mind if I smoke?" she asked.

"No," I said. "Of course not. We're outdoors." I was tempted to lecture her on the dangers of cigarette smoking, but decided it wasn't my place. Nor was it the time.

Ellie inhaled deeply, and twirled the used match between her thumb and index finger.

"Ellie, I don't want to pressure you. But you did ask that we meet this morning. Both you girls are cutting school today?"

"Yes," Rhet said. She looked at Ellie. "She's my

bad influence." She laughed lightly to let her friend know she wasn't being serious.

"Well, I hate to be an accomplice to this crime," I said, "but here I am. What's on your mind, Ellie? You left a note in my friend's raincoat at school. I took it seriously when you said you'd be here this morning because, like it or not, I have become involved with you and others in your family. Why don't you tell me what brings us here today. Believe me, I will do nothing to cause you trouble, or to hurt you. My goal is to get to the bottom of your father's murder. You can trust me. You can speak freely with me."

It looked as though she was about to open up. But three young people dressed in garish clothing— was it Halloween?—appeared and began to perform for those of us in the plaza that sunny morning. One played the guitar; the other two combined dance and mime to tell a story of sorts. I might have enjoyed watching their performance had I not felt annoyance at their intrusion. The girls watched the troupe with interest; I wondered whether that was the end of any serious conversation. It was Rhet who directed everyone's attention back to the table. She said to her friend, "Go on, Ellie. Get it off your chest. You can trust Mrs. Fletcher. Tell her everything."

The words came from Ellie's mouth as though a tape recorder was playing them back. "She didn't do it. My mother and godmother hate you. They'd kill me if they knew I was here this morning. My mother went down to Los Angeles. Nancy had a business meeting in Oakland."

I glanced to where George had taken up his position behind the greenery. I could barely see him, but knowing he was there was comforting. I turned my attention to Ellie. "When you say she didn't do it, you mean your stepmother, Kimberly."

"I never called Kimberly my stepmother. I always called her mom."

"Tell me how you know she didn't kill your father, Ellie. This might be painful for you to speak about, but—"

"It doesn't hurt anymore," the young girl said. Her face was now set in determination, as though she had summoned up every ounce of steel in her body to get through what she was about to say. "Kimberly is in prison, and she shouldn't be."

"I agree with you," I said.

"You've been visiting Kimberly in prison, haven't you?"

"Yes. How did *you* know that?"

"I heard my mother and Nancy talking about it. Nancy said she told you off the other day at your hotel."

I smiled. "I suppose 'telling me off' pretty much sums it up. May I ask you a question, Ellie?"

"Sure." She sipped her lemonade.

"Why do you live with Nancy and not with your mother?"

"Because my mother doesn't want me." She said

it so flatly, so matter-of-factly that my heart hurt for her.

"How is Kimberly, Mrs. Fletcher?" Ellie asked. She started to cry, silent tears running down her full cheeks. Rhet put her arm around her.

"Kimberly is doing as well as can be expected, I suppose. Prison is a terrible place to be. But she seems determined to make the best of it, and to leave it as soon as possible. I'm dedicated to helping her do that." I paused and scrutinized Ellie's face. "You love Kimberly, don't you?"

The tears continued. "I love her very much. I wish she had been my mother."

"Do you think your love for her is clouding your judgment about her guilt?" I asked.

As she wiped her tears with the back of her hands, a defiant expression crossed her face again. She sat up straight, looked me in the eye, and said, "No, Mrs. Fletcher. It isn't that I don't think she killed my father, I *know* she didn't."

"How do you know, Ellie? This is the time to tell me. I'm working with a good friend from Scotland Yard. He doesn't believe Kimberly killed your father, either. If you have any information, any specific knowledge that will help us, please tell me now. I don't know how much longer I can stay in San Francisco and pursue this. I need help. I need *your* help."

Ellie thought for a moment, then looked at Rhet, who nodded her head in encouragement. Ellie again fixed on me, drew a deep breath, and said, "The

Jessica Fletcher and Donald Bain

night my father died, I was awake upstairs in the house. I heard my dad's car pull into the driveway. I looked out the window and saw the car go into the garage. I thought it was Kimberly driving because just before it went into the garage, I had a quick glimpse of the driver. She had short blond hair just like Kimberly. But then I went downstairs and didn't see Kimberly there. All I saw were Nancy and my mother."

"Did you think it was strange?" I asked.

"Sure I did. But when I started to ask questions, they yelled at me and told me to go back upstairs. I was really afraid of Nancy. I always have been. So I did what they told me, and fell asleep. The next morning, I woke up and went downstairs to look in the garage. The car was gone. I asked my mother about it. She told me I must have been dreaming. I know I wasn't dreaming, Mrs. Fletcher. I saw the car arrive, and I saw Kimberly driving it. Or, at least I thought it was Kimberly."

"But I take it you're now convinced it wasn't," I said.

"That's right. I think the woman driving the car that night was Nancy."

"And what makes you think that?"

"Because just about that time, Nancy was being treated for cancer. She was getting chemotherapy, which made her lose her hair."

I sat back and cocked my head. "She wore a wig during that period?"

"Yes. They got all the cancer, and her own hair

234

eventually grew back. But when my father was killed, Nancy had a couple of blond wigs. Different styles."

I thought of Norman Lana and the blond wig on the mannequin in his bedroom closet. I thought of the wig I'd purchased a few years ago in New York in order to elude the police until I had time to extricate myself from a case with which I'd inadvertently become involved.

Wigs everywhere.

Blond hair.

Someone with blond hair had murdered Mark Steffer.

Kimberly Steffer had blond hair.

Nancy Antonio had blond wigs of varying styles.

And Norman Lana would pass for a woman in his blond wig and the right clothes.

"What color hair does your mother have, Ellie?" I asked.

"Reddish."

"Oh."

"But she sometimes wears wigs. She has a bunch of them. Black. Real red. Blond."

"Blond."

She nodded. "Here," she said, handing me a plastic supermarket bag.

"What's this?" I asked.

"One of Nancy's blond wigs."

"Oh."

"I thought you might want to see it."

"I—yes, of course I'd like to see it. More lemonade?"

"No," they said.

"Anything else?" I asked.

Ellie stood. "My birthday is day after tomorrow," she announced.

"How nice," I said.

"You know what present I want most, Mrs. Fletcher?"

"No."

"Get Kimberly out of jail so she can come home. That's all I want."

The two girls started walking away.

"Ellie," I said.

They stopped and turned.

"Come back."

They stood over me at the table. I looked down at the wig in my hands, then up at Ellie, and smiled. "Could you get free to call me at the Westin St. Francis tonight, Ellie?"

"Sure. Why?"

"I don't know if what I plan to do will pan out. But if it does, it might make your birthday wish a reality."

Their widened eyes mirrored what they were thinking.

"Call me tonight." I wrote down the hotel's number. "By nine. Okay?"

"Okay," Ellie said.

They walked away and disappeared from the square.

George rejoined me. The three street performers were now playing their act exclusively for us. We watched their creative storytelling for a few minutes until George dropped a dollar bill in the hat on the ground in front of them, and they moved on to another table.

"So, Jessica, what transpired?"

"Someone with blond hair killed Mark Steffer."

He laughed. "We already know that."

"No we don't. We know it if Kimberly Steffer did it. But she *didn't* do it."

"And?"

"Someone who wanted very much to make it look as though she killed her husband did a good job of making him, or her, look like Kimberly. Good enough to convince a jury, at least."

"*Him,* or her?"

"If you weren't insistent upon playing cat and mouse with me about last night, you'd understand. Buy me another cappuccino and I'll explain. But you go first. *Where were you last night?*"

Chapter Twenty

"You look surprised, Jess," George said.

"I have to admit I am. Not that there's any reason for you not to have dinner with Bobby McCormick. But he is, after all, the reporter who followed the Kimberly Steffer trial so closely. I would have thought—"

He raised his eyebrows into question marks, something I'm physically unable to do.

"I would have thought that you'd have told me of your plans to be with him." Was I sounding irrational?

His only response was to nod, which said he was waiting to hear what else I had to say.

"George, please don't misunderstand. I'm not implying that you have any obligation to keep me informed of your whereabouts. But it was Bobby McCormick you had dinner with. You know how interested I'd be in that. And, I must admit, I can't help but wonder why I wasn't invited."

George sipped his cappuccino, and so did I. We'd decided to linger in Ghirardelli Square and had replenished our coffees.

"Well?" I said.

He smiled. "Jessica, I know exactly how you feel. And maybe I was insensitive to your needs in this regard. It is your case, this Kimberly Steffer matter."

"I'm not claiming proprietary interest, George."

"I know you're not. The truth is, I needed to learn some things to help you, to help *us*, with this case. I thought Mr. McCormick would open up more to me—than to you."

"Guy talk?" I asked.

George laughed.

I couldn't help but join in. "Okay," I said. "I'm not nearly as upset as I probably appeared. Let's just forget it." Which I hoped he wouldn't do.

"I'm afraid we can't do that, Jessica."

"Why?" I asked, pleased.

"I'm happy to tell you why. After a couple of glasses of Glenlivet—by God, that stuff is good; if it weren't such a bloody fortune back home—I convinced Mr. McCormick to run another story about Kimberly. Sort of a follow-up."

"A follow-up? Based upon what? Reporters usually don't resurrect an old story unless there's a new angle."

"Ah, but there is."

"Me?" I asked. "Because I'm involved?"

"No, dear lady. *Me.*"

"You? What do you mean?"

"What I mean is that he is going to write that I, a high-ranking Scotland Yard inspector, have decided that Miss Kimberly Steffer has been wrongly accused of the murder of her husband. Not only that, the article will point out that I am in San Francisco to prove her innocence to the world."

"You are?"

"I am as far as the readers of Mr. McCormick's newspaper are concerned. And, hopefully, find the real murderer."

"I—"

"Most important, Jessica, it will take the focus off you. I've been worried about what happened to you on the bridge that morning. I don't think it was coincidental. But McCormick's story might make whoever is after you realize they're after the wrong man—the wrong woman. I'm the one they should have tried to push off the Golden Gate Bridge. I want to expedite things. I feel we're close, yet so far from getting to the truth. I can taste it. Hopefully, someone—*the* someone responsible for Mark Steffer's death—will take the bait and try to get rid of this snoopy Scotsman. If it works—bingo! That is the correct American expression, isn't it?"

I nodded.

"Now, if I'd told you about my plan before meeting with Mr. McCormick, you'd surely have tried to talk me out of it. Correct me if I'm wrong."

"No. You're right. I'll even admit that I like your scheme. I see why you're held in such high regard. A veritable Sherlock Holmes."

"And you, Jessica? My Dr. Watson?"

"Pleased to be."

He lifted his almost empty, foam-rimmed, oversize cappuccino mug to mine. "To the new firm of Sutherland and Fletcher. Or Fletcher and Sutherland. Whichever you prefer. Cheers."

"Cheers. Now what, Mr. Holmes?"

"Let's see. I presume Mr. Bobby McCormick has already filed his story, hopefully in time for today's late edition. I suggest we sit tight, just as we are. Enjoy the sunshine and this pretty city. I have a few hours of work to log, and a series of faxes to get off to Scotland Yard before the day escapes me. Your plans?"

"I was going to the San Francisco Zen Center. I understand they have a fabulous restaurant there. Greens, it's called. The views across the bay to the Golden Gate are breathtaking, according to Camille. Not up your alley, though, George. Strictly vegetarian."

"Then, I won't feel deprived not accompanying you. My only concern is having you out of my sight. Why not invite Camille to join you?"

"Don't be silly, George. Not much can happen in broad daylight."

"As I recall, your incident on the bridge didn't happen at midnight."

"Beside the point. I'm looking forward to lunching by myself today."

"Then, take this." He handed me a beeper.

"Beep me at some point just to check in," he said. "If it goes off, you'll know I'm beeping you, since I'm the only one who knows your number. Go immediately to a phone and call the number that you read on the beeper. That's where I can be reached.

Your beeper number, by the way, is three-three-four. My number is five-seven-eight. Beep me if you need help, or just want to talk."

"I'll feel like a doctor. Or a drug dealer."

"A thin line between them at times. Let's meet back at the hotel for afternoon tea at four."

"Sounds wonderful."

George eyed the bag containing the wig Ellie had given me. "What do you make of that?" he asked.

I shrugged.

"Want me to take it back with me to the hotel?"

I was about to say yes but changed my mind. "No, that's okay," I said. "I'll just put it in here." I shoved the plastic supermarket bag into my dependable fake Chanel bag that I'd been lugging around San Francisco since arriving. Inside was also Kimberly's diary; I wanted to read portions of it again over lunch in the hope of something jumping out at me from the page. Some overlooked clue, some sudden insight that would help put the pieces of the puzzle together.

We shared a cab; first stop, the Zen Center at Fort Mason, originally a depot for war supplies to the Pacific during World War II. The monstrous, three-story, yellow-stucco building housed several small museums, as well as the restaurant, Greens. I watched as the cab pulled away to take him back to the hotel.

The Zen Center was a bit too esoteric for me. I quickly walked through two of the four museums, stopping to admire little. Fortunately, it was already lunchtime. The contemporary artwork gracing the walls of Greens was far more pleasing to my eye than what I'd seen in the museums. So was the splendid view from my waterside table. I ordered a mineral water and lentil salad, took out Kimberly's diary, and read the page to which I happened to open first.

One of my favorite songs has always been one sung by the blues singer, Dinah Washington. It's called "What a Difference A Day Makes." I'm living proof of that. Just the night before my arrest for Mark's murder, life was so simple. I remember sitting at the salon getting my hair cut and thinking about how wonderful my life was. Yes, Mark and I had our problems. But at that stage of our marriage, I was in denial. I wanted to believe that everything was perfect between us, that his coming home late, or never at all, was innocent. That he really was playing poker with his buddies, or hanging around the restaurant for a nightcap after closing up. My instincts told me otherwise, but I had to have faith.

I didn't want to change my life. I could barely muster up the courage to cut my hair, let alone instigate a divorce. I remember being totally shocked while looking in the mirror at the salon, my flowing blond hair on the floor at my feet. The cut made me look wiser, more sophisticated, like someone to be reckoned with, respected. After the initial shock, I liked the look. But I feared Mark's reaction. I stopped the car several times before driving home to make sure it looked okay, to comb it one more time, to spray a few strands into place.

Of course, Mark wasn't home. Ironically, he never did see my haircut, see the "new me." In fact, not many people did except in the newspapers. One was allegedly the cabdriver, who testified he'd picked me up at the mall and delivered me to the health club. I was at the club that evening, and the manager on duty affirmed that I'd been there that night. But I hadn't taken a cab there. Yes, I had been at the mall that day. Yes, the American Express receipts showed I'd bought a lipstick and two eye shadows from the Clinique counter. Yes, it was my handwriting.

But I'd driven from the mall to the health club. I did not leave Mark's car at the mall with his body stuffed in the trunk. I was framed. I was set up.

What a difference a day made.

I stuffed the diary into the bag, took out the blond wig, and looked it over until finding a label. Written on it were a series of numbers, and HOUSE OF WIGS: SAUSALITO.

Bingo!

I thought of George and smiled. Should I beep him to let him know of my whereabouts? Instead, I paid the check, and bounced down the stairs to the street where I found a cab idling.

"You wouldn't know where the House of Wigs is would you?" I asked enthusiastically as I opened the door to the cab.

"Yes, ma'am," the driver sang. "The Sausalito Mall. Been driving these streets twenty-four years." I immediately liked him, not to mention the fact that something told me I was about to hit gold.

Chapter Twenty-one

The Wonderful World of Wigs was a more elegant shop than its overblown name suggested. It sat along with a hundred other shops and stores, some small, some large, in the Sausalito Mall, which looked like any other mall except that it was in California. Everything looks different in California.

I looked in the window at the display of wigs on white plastic heads, the heads looking like hard-boiled eggs. There was no one else in the shop, so I went in: "No, thank you," I said in response to an offer of help from a middle-aged woman with a Dolly Parton blond hairdo that I assumed was a wig, not because it looked like one but because she worked in a wig store. That sort of reasoning would never hold up in court.

"Just browsing," I said pleasantly, perusing the dozens of wigs on display. Mirrors everywhere flashed my image back at me from myriad angles.

After a few minutes, the clerk—was she the owner? I wondered—said, "Sure I can't be of help?"

"Well, maybe you can," I said. "But I'm not in

the market for a wig. I'm interested in this one." I opened my bag, pulled out the wig Ellie Steffer had given me that morning, and handed it to her.

"What about it?" she asked.

"I suppose the first question I have is whether this particular wig was purchased at this store."

"Oh, yes. It has our label sewn into it. See?" She pointed to it.

"Of course," I said. "Silly of me not to have noticed."

"Is there something wrong with it?" she asked.

I was tempted to comment that it might have been worn by a murderer. Instead, I replied, "Not at all. It's a lovely blond wig. You wouldn't—I suppose you wouldn't—"

"Your face is familiar."

"Oh?"

She snapped her fingers a few times, and screwed up her face. "Jessica Fletcher. The mystery writer."

"Uh-huh."

"What a pleasure." She extended her hand.

"Thank you," I said, taking it.

"What did you want? You said I probably wouldn't have something." Before I could respond, she added, "Anything you want, Mrs. Fletcher. Just name it. I've read some of your books. They're wonderful. You're wonderful."

"That's very kind of you."

"I read about what happened to you on the bridge. Terrible. So many sickos running around these days. Business is down here because women are afraid to go to malls. Not that we have many problems at this one. It's very well run. But still—"

"You wouldn't by chance have a record of when this wig was purchased?" I asked. "And by whom?"

"I think I can get that information for you. We're a service-oriented store. It's the only way to stay in business. Give service. We keep careful records on all our customers. It's all in our computer. Don't know what we'd do without the computer. We used to keep records by hand until we—"

"I'd really appreciate it," I said. "I don't have much time."

"Just give me a minute, and I'll look it up for you."

I followed her to the rear of the store where the computer sat on a small neat desk. She keyed in some entries, and a series of sales records filled the screen. "See?" she said. "Each wig we sell is identified by a serial number we assign." She leaned close and peered at the screen, one finger on a key that caused the records to flow vertically. "Let me see that again."

I handed her the wig I'd brought with me.

"Oh, yes. Here we are. The number on this wig is four-ten." She continued scanning files until stopping at the one she'd sought. "That's funny," she said.

"What's funny?" I asked.

She looked up at me. "This is wrong. According to our records, number four-ten is a shoulder-length blond wig."

My heart skipped a beat. My supposition was moving closer to reality.

"Wait a minute," she said. She took the wig in her hand and ran her fingers through it, stopping to inspect a few individual strands of hair. "This wig has been cut," she said. "It's easy to see if you look closely. In its original state, when it was sold, it was shoulder-length blond. This wig has been cut shorter."

"Do your records indicate who purchased this wig?" I asked.

She returned her attention to the computer screen. "I'll need to pull up another file," she said. "Here we go. WIG NUMBER FOUR-TEN. AMERICAN EXPRESS. ROBERT FREDERICKSON."

I said nothing.

"Do you know Mr. Frederickson?" she asked.

"Yes. He's an acquaintance. Is it unusual for a man to buy a wig?"

"Oh, no. I'd say our sales are pretty much evenly divided between men and women."

"Female impersonators?"

"Some. The cast from Finocchio's and Beach Blanket Babylon are steady customers."

"I would imagine."

"But most men who buy wigs are—" She smiled knowingly. "They buy them for wives and girlfriends. You know, to change the way they look. To inject some spice, some change in their lovemaking."

"I see."

"I hope this has been helpful, Mrs. Fletcher."

"Oh, you've been very helpful Ms.—"

"Warren. June Warren. Say, Mrs. Fletcher, could I ask a favor of you?"

"One favor certainly deserves another," I replied.

"There's a bookstore in the mall. Only a few stores down. Your new book is called—?"

"Blood Relations."

"I want to buy a copy and have you autograph it for me."

"I'd be delighted."

"You watch the shop. I'll be back in ten minutes."

Fifteen minutes later I left The Wonderful World of Wigs knowing three things: That Robert Frederickson had bought a blond wig there; that someone had given it a haircut to make it shorter; and that at least one copy of my newest novel had been sold.

That latter fact paled in comparison to the meaning of the first two realities.

Chapter Twenty-two

"It's all set with Josephs," George said, sounding pleased. "He'll bring Kimberly to the restaurant."

"Wonderful."

"Ms. Steffer will be there celebrating her birthday?"

"Yes. Her mother and Nancy Antonio balked at first. But Ellie said they quickly changed their minds after receiving a call from Robert Frederickson."

"Undoubtedly, telling them I would be there."

"Undoubtedly."

The plan George Sutherland and I concocted to force Mark Steffer's killer into the open took shape over a series of meetings spanning a night and a day. We'd met up the evening of my discovery at The Wonderful World of Wigs—that Robert Frederickson had purchased a shoulder-length blond wig there, and that someone had subsequently trimmed it into a shorter version. George's imagination went into high gear.

He approached the creation of a workable scheme

like an architect planning a bridge or skyscraper, or a football coach coming up with an offense for the big game. Come to think of it, he plotted things out the way I do when planning my mystery novels: Charts linking one character with another, events interlocking and leading to an inevitable conclusion.

Of course, I'm able to control the outcome in my books. In the case of Mark Steffer's murder, George and I could only hope that what we put into play would lead to the conclusion we desired, identifying the real murderer, and by extension proving Kimberly Steffer innocent.

"Ready?" he asked.

"Ready as I'll ever be," I said. "Let's go."

The doorman whistled us a cab.

"Have you got the wig, Jess?" George asked after we'd settled in the backseat.

"Right here in my bag." I pulled it out and held it up to ambient light coming through the cab's window. "How do you think I'll look as a blond?" I asked.

"As beautiful as with your natural hair," he replied.

"You should have been a diplomat," I said, placing the wig on my head and adjusting it by touch.

"Nice," he said. "But they'll still know it's you."

"I'm sure of that. But seeing me wearing it should set a few teeth on edge."

He laughed softly. "Of that, I'm sure," he said. "Oh, yes. Of that, I'm certain."

We said little else to each other during the ride, and I contented myself with gazing out the window. I was nervous about the confrontation that was about to happen. At the same time, a sense of exhilaration took hold. If things went as planned, the Kimberly Steffer "cause" I'd taken on would be over. Over for Kimberly, over for Ellie Steffer, over for me, and over for George. Of course, I was also aware that I was embarking on another "wig caper"—shades of my New York adventure a few years ago. In that instance, I used a wig to go undetected for enough time to race home to Cabot Cove in search of the answer to a murderous question. Here, in San Francisco, I was wearing it for shock value.

Darkness shrouded the City by the Bay. It glistened through the window, the surrealistic shapes of buildings and neon signs enhanced by a mist that glazed the glass. I was so engrossed in thought, I didn't realize that George had taken my hand. It felt good.

We sat silently, the rhythm of the wipers on the windshield, the whoosh of tires on wet pavement, our regular breathing and an occasional beep of a horn the only sounds. And then, as if a film director had cued the sound track, Tony Bennett singing "I Left My Heart in San Francisco" oozed from rear speakers. Like a scene from an old-fashioned love story, I thought. George squeezed my hand and held it tighter for the rest of the trip.

Eventually, our driver pulled into the parking lot

of What's to Eat?. Precipitation had stopped; our anticipation had dramatically increased.

"George. Look," I said, pointing to a small white Toyota parked in the first row of cars. Getting out of it were Ellie and Joan Steffer, and Nancy Antonio.

"Bingo," George said. "So far, so good."

I smiled at the use of his newly acquired American expression, wondering how it would go over back home in Great Britain.

George leaned forward and placed his hand on the driver's shoulder. "Don't drop us off at the entrance just yet," he said. "Perhaps you'd be good enough to drive us about a bit."

"Sure," the driver responded. He was an older man wearing a checkered green cap and a gray wool cardigan sweater. Tired eyes said he'd seen it all.

"Take us over there," George said, indicating a far corner of the large front parking lot.

We watched from that vantage point as Robert Frederickson came through the restaurant's front door to greet Ellie, her mother and godmother. He wasn't smiling. No one was. Poor Ellie, I thought. She'd been dragged along for what promised to be a distinctly unpleasant evening at the expense of her mother and godmother. But if the evening turned out as George and I hoped, Ellie would see her birthday wish fulfilled. Kimberly Steffer would be a free woman.

After Frederickson and the new arrivals were inside, another taxi pulled into the lot.

"Is that him?" I asked.

"I'm sure it is. Yes. See? He's parked where I instructed him to park."

I nodded. "It really might work," I said.

"Hopefully. I'd still feel better if you didn't insist upon being with me," George said quietly.

"Not a chance," I said. "If you've come here to-night to deliberately put yourself in harm's way, you're going to have to put up with me at your side. I consider myself your partner. Partners stick together."

After a deep, pained sigh, he tapped the driver on the shoulder and said, "You can take us to the entrance now."

As we pulled up, we could make out Freder-ickson's strong, handsome profile through a window. George paid the driver and opened the taxi's door for me. We walked up the short yellow brick path to the front door, George humming a few bars of "We're Off to See the Wizard."

"I wish I could kick my heels three times and be home," I said.

We stepped inside and were face-to-face with Robert Frederickson.

"Good evening," George said. "I'm Scotland Yard Inspector Sutherland. I have a reservation."

Frederickson heard what George said, but his at-tention was solely on me, more accurately on my newly acquired blond hair.

"Mrs. Fletcher?" he said.

"Good evening, Mr. Frederickson. How nice to see you again."

"You look—"

"Different? Must be this wig I'm wearing. I've always wanted to be a blond. How do I look?"

"You look—" Frederickson turned to George: "You said when you made the reservation that you were bringing your niece for a birthday dinner."

"Absolutely correct," George said, his smile wide and engaging. "My niece is running late. She should be here any minute. Mrs. Fletcher is joining us to help celebrate the occasion. Perhaps we could enjoy a drink while we wait for her. You do serve alcohol?"

"Yes, but this is a—"

"A family restaurant catering to children," George said.

"That's correct." Frederickson took two menus from a rack on the wall and escorted us to the same room at the rear where I'd had lunch, evidently reserved for adult, whiskey-drinking interlopers at What's to Eat?. I looked around the main room on our way through for signs of Ellie, but didn't see her.

We were seated at a table set for six. "Enjoy your meal," Frederickson said, handing the menus to George.

"I'm sure we will," George replied. Frederickson's eyes locked with mine before he walked away and disappeared through swinging doors leading to the kitchen.

A young waitress bounced over to take our drink orders. We pretended to study the menu, although the whimsically named entrées were furthest from our minds.

"Interesting menu," George said, smiling.

"Plenty of things on it to satisfy you," I said.

"No sushi."

"No sushi."

Our waitress returned with our drinks. "These are compliments of Mr. Frederickson," she said.

"How nice," I said. I looked for him to acknowledge his gesture, but he was nowhere to be found. "Please thank him for us," I said.

Our drinks were in front of us, but the waitress continued to stand there, hands resting on small hips.

"Yes?" George said, looking up.

"Oh, I forgot. What's to eat?" I asked, turning to George. "There's a protocol in this restaurant. You have to ask 'What's to eat?' before you're allowed to order."

"That's right," the waitress said, her small, round face breaking into a Vaseline-enhanced smile.

"If I don't eat my vegetables, will I still get dessert?" George asked. I laughed. The waitress failed to see the humor.

"We're waiting for the rest of our party before we order," I said. "Besides, I haven't had a chance to scan the menu. So many—wonderful things from which to choose."

"I'll be back," said the waitress.

The minute she was gone, I looked through an archway into the larger main dining room. Frederickson had led Ellie, Nancy, and Joan to a corner table that afforded one of the chairs a view of us. Where had they been all this time? I wondered. Ellie was seated in the chair facing us. Our eyes met, but she quickly looked away.

"Don't turn, George," I whispered, "but they're sitting in the main dining room. Behind you."

"Ah, hah. Keep your eye on them, Jess."

Our waitress returned.

"It seems the rest of our party has been held up," George said. "I suppose we should order." Once we had and the waitress was gone, George lifted his gin on the rocks to my white wine. "To Kimberly Steffer," he whispered.

"Yes. To Kimberly. Hopefully, it won't be a wasted toast."

We made nervous small talk while waiting for our dinners, and for the next phase of our plan to kick in. I suffered a sudden twinge of apprehension. No, make that downright fear. George had decided on this scheme for two reasons: One, to flush out Mark Steffer's real killer. And two, to shift the spotlight from me to him. It was that second reason that caused me concern. Bobby McCormick's newspaper article made it clear that George Sutherland, Scotland Yard investigator, was in San Francisco to clear Kimberly Steffer's name. Which meant, of course, that the real murderer might decide to do away with George Sutherland. Right there and then? At What's to Eat?

But how might such an attempt on his life play out?

Poison in our food and drinks?

"George," I said, placing my hand on his arm. "Maybe it isn't such a good idea for us to be drinking and eating here."

"Why? I'm sure the food isn't terribly good, but—"

"Because Mr. Frederickson and whoever else he's involved with might decide to add an extra spice, an extra ingredient that isn't called for in the original recipe."

"Yes. I see what you mean. But highly unlikely, wouldn't you agree?"

"How is your gin?"

"Excellent."

"No funny tastes?"

"No."

"Good."

I looked again at Ellie. Poor girl, I thought. A true victim.

"What time do you have?" I asked.

"Almost eight. Josephs and Kimberly are obviously tied up. Traffic, perhaps. Or maybe Josephs had trouble getting her out of prison."

"I thought he'd received permission to bring her here."

"Even so, there's always the infernal paperwork. I just hope the judge who issued the order hasn't changed his mind. It took courage on his part to do it, to say nothing of a surprisingly creative move for a judge. I also have to give Josephs credit for presenting a compelling reason to the court. I give that credit reluctantly, however."

"I hope they show soon," I said. "This waiting is getting to me."

"Any sign of Frederickson reappearing?" George asked.

"No. He seated them but hasn't come back to the table."

"I wonder what he's up to."

"As long as it isn't—"

The sight of Kimberly Steffer and Detective Walter Josephs entering the room stopped me in mid-sentence. Kimberly wore a dark scarf wrapped around her head, and oversize sunglasses. I checked Ellie's table. I could see Nancy Antonio's shoulder and a portion of Joan Steffer's head. If they noticed the new arrivals, they didn't indicate it by any sudden movements.

George stood and motioned for Josephs to come to our table. Kimberly kept her head down, and stayed close to the detective as they crossed the room.

"Sit down, sit down," George said, holding out a chair for Kimberly to my left, which presented only her profile to Ellie and the others.

"Sorry we're late," Josephs said, grabbing a roll from a basket and biting off a hunk. "Damn judge changed rules at the last minute. Couldn't bring her here without a half dozen other cops trailing. Two of 'em are taking a table in that other room. The other four are outside watching every exit in case Ms. Steffer here decides to do something stupid."

"You don't have to worry about that," Kimberly said softly. She started to remove her glasses, but George suggested she keep them on. "Too early for us to spring *that* surprise," he said gently.

"You look wonderful, Kimberly," I said, patting her hand.

"Thanks, Mrs. Fletcher." Her voice was tense, tight.

"Everything's going to be all right," I said. "Just try and relax."

Small grayish steaks, garnished with cooked cherry tomatoes and home fries, were placed before George and me. He'd ordered his black-and-blue, but it looked like both were cooked well-done. Not surprising. Kids always like their meat that way.

"Ready to order?" George asked Kimberly and Josephs.

"Yeah," Josephs replied. "What's that thing you're eating?"

"A steak."

"It is?"

"So they say."

"Lemme see a menu," Josephs told the waitress, who sighed and went in search of one.

"Actually, it might be better if—"

My grip on George's wrist stopped him from completing what he'd started to say. I was looking through the arch at Ellie's table where her mother and Nancy Antonio had turned in their chairs and were staring at us. "A little anxiety in the other room," I said.

"Oh?"

"You were saying?"

"I was saying that it might make sense to hasten things up a bit."

"So?" Josephs said.

"So, Detective, I think it would be better to skip your main courses and get right to dessert."

"How come?" Josephs asked, eating another roll.

"Because according to our astute Mrs. Fletcher's instincts, it's time to push things forward."

"Time for the birthday cake," I said. To Kimberly: "Are you ready to celebrate your birthday?"

"Yes, even though it isn't."

"Then let's do it."

"Do what?" Josephs asked.

George caught the waitress's eye and waved her to the table. "Our late-arriving friends have already eaten elsewhere. But we're ready for the cake now."

"You don't want dinner?" the waitress said to Josephs and Kimberly.

They shook their heads. Josephs grabbed another roll before the waitress took away the bread basket.

George motioned everyone to lean closer. "Here's what happens next," he said in a stage whisper. "I've ordered a birthday cake for 'my niece.' Obviously, my niece isn't here. More to the point, the only nieces I have are back in Scotland, and I didn't think it wise, or cost-effective to fly them in for the occasion. At any rate, I requested that the cake not have a name on it. They treated it as a strange request, almost demanded that a name appear. But I held fast. The cake will simply say 'Happy Birthday,' and will contain thirteen candles."

"Thirteen?" Josephs asked, looking at each person at the table, his expression disbelief.

George ignored him. "It is Mr. Frederickson's policy to personally join in the singing of 'Happy Birthday' to everyone so honored in his establishment. Probably, a thwarted theatrical career. No matter. He will come to the table and join in. Is everyone ready?"

We nodded. My stomach tightened. I felt Kimberly tense next to me, and gave her a reassuring smile. I looked to where Ellie sat with her mother and godmother. Their dinners had been served, but they seemed more interested in our table than what was on their plates. In a moment, their interest would be elevated tenfold.

The kitchen door opened. Our waitress came through it carrying a small cake. Candles flickered and glowed, their flames bending with the breeze caused by her forward motion. I checked Ellie's table again. All three women were watching, along with dozens of other diners.

Robert Frederickson stood in the open kitchen doorway. He seemed unsure whether to follow the waitress and lend his voice to the singing. George noticed his ambivalence and waved for him to join the festivities. Other waiters and waitresses on their way to take part in the ritual singing that was part of their jobs detoured in Frederickson's direction and, taking his arms and laughing, propelled him toward us.

When they arrived, George motioned for the waitress to place the cake in front of Kimberly.

"Time to take off the scarf and sunglasses, Kimberly," I said.

She slowly removed them, raised her lovely face, and looked directly at Frederickson, the warm candlelight from the cake rendering her natural beauty even more apparent. A waiter started the song: ". . . *Happy Birthday dear Kimberly, happy birthday to you.*"

All eyes were on Frederickson as we harmonized with the chorus, badly, I might add. His mouth was open, but no musical sounds came from it. His eyes were large dishes. Together with his gaping mouth, he had the appearance of a handsome fish.

The waiters and waitresses drifted away.

"Time to blow out the candles," I said. "Make a wish, Kimberly."

She closed her eyes tight, as though trying to shut out the horror of what she'd been through. Tears leaked through the creases. I stood and faced Frederickson, whose expression said it all. "Yes, Mr. Frederickson," I said. "It's Kimberly Steffer."

"What the hell is—?"

"What's going on," I said, "is *this.*" I removed my wig and held it out as an offering to him.

He recoiled, as though the wig were hot.

"I don't blame you for not wanting to touch it—again," I said.

His forced smile was painfully painted on.

"This is the wig you bought as part of your efforts to frame Kimberly Steffer for the murder of her husband, Mark Steffer."

George stood, adding, "You should stay out of the haircutting business, Mr. Frederickson. Not a very appealing cut you gave it."

I turned in the direction of Ellie's table. She, her mother, and her godmother were looking right at us. I held the wig high for them to see. "Maybe they'd like to join us," I said to Detective Josephs.

He went to their table. We saw him flash his badge, and engage in unheard conversation. The three women slowly got up and followed him to our table. Two men in suits, whom I assumed were the detectives sitting in the other room, suggested to the few diners in our room that they leave. Others in the large main dining room had become aware that something was up, and had come to the archways separating the rooms. The detective politely asked them to take their seats and to ignore what was going on. That task completed, they joined us.

"What is this nonsense?" Nancy Antonio asked, her large face in a sneer.

"I wouldn't call it 'nonsense,'" George said. "You know Mrs. Fletcher, of course."

"Hello," I said.

She ignored me, turned to Frederickson, and said, "What have you done?"

He extended his hands in a feeble plea for understanding.

"I imagine you look rather fetching as a blond," George said to Nancy. "Jessica." I handed the wig to her. "Try it on for size," George said.

She stood with her arms crossed over her ample bosom. "Where did you get that?" she demanded.

"I gave it to them," Ellie said in a voice so soft it was barely audible.

"*You?*" Joan Steffer blurted.

"What are you trying to prove?" Nancy asked.

"Your guilt in the murder of Mark Steffer," I said. "Go ahead, Ms. Antonio. We're all waiting."

Her defiant stance came as no surprise to me after my run-in with her in the hotel lobby. She pulled herself to full height and grabbed the wig from my hands. Joan Steffer, whose expression was sheer panic, turned to leave, but the two detectives blocked her path. "Stay around, Mrs. Steffer," said George. "The show isn't over yet."

Ellie Steffer stood between her mother and her godmother. She and Kimberly had been looking at each other ever since the confrontation began. Now she took steps toward Kimberly.

"Ellie, stay away from her," her mother ordered.

Ellie and Kimberly cried as they threw their arms about each other.

We all looked at Nancy Antonio, who continued to hold the wig. "Well, Ms. Antonio?" George said.

Her mouth was a slash of anger as she pulled on the wig. "Satisfied?" she snarled.

"As a matter of fact, we're not," I said. "I'd like to see it on Mrs. Steffer."

George and I exchanged glances. We'd discussed the trying on of the wig before entering the restaurant, and concluded that Nancy Antonio was too large a woman to have been mistaken for Kimberly Steffer, no matter what wig she wore. Joan Steffer was another story. She was Kimberly's height, and shared her slender build.

Nancy Antonio yanked the wig from her head and fairly threw it at her. "Go on, Joan," she said. "Give 'em a show."

"I will not," Joan said firmly.

"Why not?" The question was asked by Ellie, who now faced her mother. They were no more than a foot from each other. "Why not, Mom?" she repeated. "Afraid?"

"Afraid? Of what?"

"Of the truth coming out?"

"You—" I thought for a moment Joan was about to physically attack her daughter. The intense dislike for each other was palpable.

Joan forced a laugh. A guffaw actually. "Here," she said, pulling on the wig. "Satisfied?"

"Yes," I said.

George had left the room during the argument over the blond wig. He returned, followed by another gentleman who I knew was the cabdriver, Phillipe Fernandez, the one who'd testified at Kimberly's trial that he'd picked her up at the mall, the one with the thick eyeglasses, the one who'd driven me one day in San Francisco. We'd paid him to wait outside until fetched by George.

"Could this be the woman you drove from the mall to the health club, Mr. Fernandez?" George asked, pointing to Joan Steffer.

"That's her," Fernandez said loudly. "That is the woman."

"Sure it wasn't her?" I asked, indicating Kimberly.

Mr. Fernandez leaned closer to Kimberly, then took in Joan Steffer again. "It's her," he said, his eyes focused on Joan.

Throughout these exchanges, Robert Frederickson stood silently. He seemed to have regained a modicum of composure. His facial muscles had relaxed, and his pose was nonchalant. George and I turned to face him.

"Very clever, Mrs. Fletcher, Inspector Sutherland. I'm impressed."

"Impressed that we're pointing the finger of guilt at you, Mr. Frederickson?" George asked.

He laughed. "You're looking at the wrong person," he said.

"No, we're not. You killed my husband, and a wonderful young girl's father." Kimberly's voice was soft, its impact loud. She stood and faced Frederickson. As she spoke, her voice gained in volume and anger. "I've spent a good part of my life paying for your horrible, horrible crime," she said. "In jail. I woke up every morning to the cold, dank reality of a prison cell while all of you wake up in your lovely homes, listening to the singing of birds, smelling a fresh-brewed cappuccino. Maybe a long, leisurely shower, or a Jacuzzi. Time spent choosing what to wear—silk or cashmere today, blue suit or brown? But I knew that when you looked at yourselves in the mirror, you knew that underneath your good looks were evil people.

"Ironic, isn't it, that I preferred to wake up as me, in a prison cell, rather than you and the lies your lives represent. I thought of you every morning, Robert. And you, Nancy, and Joan. Because I didn't have proof that you killed Mark, I could only take comfort in knowing that I hadn't. I didn't kill anyone. *But you did!*" She said it directly to Robert Frederickson.

Frederickson wasn't quite as composed as when Kimberly had started talking. He fidgeted with his hands and looked nervously from face to face. "Look," he said, "you two have done your snooping around and figured out a few things. But you're talking to the wrong person. You've got the ones you want right in front of you." He looked first at Nancy Antonio, then at Joan Steffer.

"But you bought the wig," I said.

"Prove it!"

"As easily done as said," I said. "The Wonderful World of Wigs, Mr. Frederickson. You purchased a shoulder-length blond wig there. We've entered the computer age. You should know that, being a successful businessman. You purchased this wig using your American Express card. Every wig paid for by credit card at that shop is recorded. The moral, I suppose, is to never leave home *with* it."

He said nothing.

I continued: "Must have been quite a shock to learn that Kimberly had her hair cut shorter that day, and not just a trim. A whole new look. That left you no time to buy a new wig. Not on the eve of the big night."

"Excuse me," Frederickson said, "I have a restaurant to run." Detective Josephs stepped in front of him as he took a step toward the main dining room. "Hey, look," Frederickson said, indicating people in both archways watching what was unfolding in our room. "We're making a scene here."

"That's the last thing you should be concerned about, Mr. Frederickson," George said.

"So I bought a damned blond wig," Frederickson said. "That doesn't make me a murderer." He looked at Nancy Antonio. "I bought it for her."

"Shut up, Bob," Nancy said.

I held up my hands and said, "Let me tell you what *I* think happened here." I looked to Ellie. This was going to be difficult for her to hear. "The night of Mark's murder was one of his weekly scheduled visitations with Ellie. He was to pick her up at her godmother's house at five for dinner, and return her home by nine. It was a weekly event. Joan, her mother, was there. As usual, she instructed Ellie to wait outside for her father. She did that and—"

"Can I finish the story, Mrs. Fletcher?" Ellie asked. She stood close to Kimberly; they held hands. Kimberly smiled warmly at her. "You told me to wait outside like you always did," Ellie said, looking at her mother. Her voice was strong and clear. "So I did. But Daddy never came. I went back inside to tell you, Mom, but you said Daddy had called and said he couldn't make it because of some business emergency. That didn't make any sense to me. Daddy never did that. He always showed up. But I couldn't ask you because it would make you mad. Everything always makes you mad. So I went back outside and waited and waited until it got dark. I remember feeling so alone and angry. I even thought that maybe I'd never see my father again. I said that to you, Mom, when I finally gave up waiting and came back inside. But you laughed at me." She paused for a few seconds to wipe tears from her face. So did I.

"I couldn't sleep," she continued. "Later that night I heard the garage door open. I got up and looked out my window. I saw Daddy's car being driven into the garage. I thought it might be Daddy, but then saw that the driver had blond hair. I came downstairs and saw Nancy. And you, Mom. You looked so different wearing that blond wig. Remember? You saw me leaning over the banister and started screaming at me. Nancy grabbed the wig off your head and told me to go back to bed.

"I had plans to go shopping with Kimberly at the mall that morning. You'd said it was okay for me to do that. You even encouraged me to go with her. That was really strange because you were usually against my seeing her. While I was getting dressed that morning, I heard the car start up in the garage.

I looked out my window and saw you drive off, Mom."

Now she started to cry openly.

"What I didn't know was that my daddy was in the trunk. You killed him that night. You and Mr. Frederickson and Nancy." She buried her face in her hands, and Kimberly hugged her.

"I need to finish," she said, taking a deep, prolonged breath. "I remembered at breakfast, you said I couldn't go to the mall, Mom, because you said Kimberly had called to cancel and was worried about where Daddy was. I wanted to call her, but of course you said I couldn't. You hadn't told me the real reason I wouldn't be seeing Kimberly, that Daddy was dead, and that Kimberly would be blamed for his murder."

Now I took over: "I know what happened next," I said. "I know it from the diary Kimberly has kept since going to prison. She gave me that diary when I visited her there. What you'd actually done that morning, Joan, was to call Kimberly to say that Ellie couldn't join you. You told her Ellie was sick and still sleeping. A lie. But then you encouraged Kimberly to buy Ellie a little something to make her feel better about having missed out on her mall excursion with you. According to what Kimberly wrote in her diary, you sounded anxious that she buy Ellie a gift. A big change in what had been your earlier attitudes toward her and her relationship with Ellie. In any event, she took your suggestion and went to the mall in search of a gift for 'the sick child.'

"Joan, you drove the car to the mall that morning and parked it in a remote spot in the lot, locked it, and went inside. Several hours later you called a taxi service. This gentleman, Mr. Fernandez, picked you up and dropped you off at the health club. Knowing that Kimberly worked out at that same club, you went there hoping the cabdriver would recall having dropped you off there. You'd told Mr. Fernandez that your car had broken down at the mall, which was why you needed the lift. Of course, you were wearing the blond wig Mr. Frederickson purchased for you, and that had been cut to a shorter length to match Kimberly's short haircut the day before.

"When Mark hadn't returned home the night before, Kimberly called Ellie to see if he might be there. Joan told Kimberly that Ellie was still sick and in bed. Meanwhile, Mr. Frederickson here called the police to inform them that his business partner hadn't shown up at the restaurant, and that he was worried because he wasn't answering his beeper, either. The police found Mark's car at the mall, and arrested Kimberly as a prime suspect in the murder.

"Everything was going smoothly for the three of you," I continued. "Kimberly did shop at the mall that day, charging several items on her charge card, including a pretty shirt for Ellie. She shopped because you urged her to, Mrs. Steffer, lying when you said Ellie was sick and would appreciate a nice gift. So Kimberly did as you suggested, just as planned. The night you actually killed Mark also went smoothly. You, Ms. Antonio, got Mark to agree to meet you to talk about some bogus traumatic situation Ellie was undergoing. You thought this lie wouldn't be noticed. But Ellie overheard your call to Mark and it puzzled her. What traumatic situation was she facing? None as far as she knew. But she rationalized it away. She was so used to dysfunctional family life that nothing was beyond possibility.

"Mark loved his daughter dearly. When he received that call, he readily agreed to meet with you. How sad. A loving father comes to discuss his daughter's problems with someone he assumes has her best interest in mind, but instead faces a murderess. Is that when you shot him, Nancy, and dragged him into the car. Ellie saw you arrive at home that night wearing the blond wig. You pulled the car into the garage. What happened then, Ms. Antonio? Did you stuff his body into the trunk all by yourself, or did Joan help you?"

George, Detective Josephs, and I took in Frederickson, Joan Steffer, and Nancy Antonio. Their reactions to what had been said were markedly different. Joan Steffer, who hadn't exhibited much bravado when the confrontation started, had now assumed a nasty, defiant edge. Robert Frederickson looked as though someone had pricked his confidence balloon, not sure whether to run, cry, or both. Nancy Antonio's posture was what interested me most. This formidable woman's face had sagged and softened. There was a vulnerability in her large brown-green eyes that wasn't there when the evening started. She was staring at Frederickson as though expecting him to do something to put an end to all this. To snap his fingers and take her away from it.

I turned to Ellie, who was now composed. "Ellie," I asked, "do you know any reason your mother, your godmother, and Mr. Frederickson would have wanted to kill your father?"

"I didn't kill anybody," Frederickson said sharply. "All I did was buy the wig for them because Nancy asked me to. There's no crime in buying a wig."

"Are you saying that it was these two women who murdered Mark Steffer?" I asked.

"I suppose so."

"You bastard," Joan Steffer snarled.

Frederickson held up his hands in mock defense. "Hey, no need to get testy, Joan. All I know is that if what Mrs. Fletcher and her Scotland Yard friend says is true, you've got yourself a pretty big problem."

"Bob," Nancy Antonio said in a surprisingly soft voice. "Please."

"Please, hell. I'm not taking the rap for anybody."

"How can you say that?" Nancy said.

George and I looked at each other. What we'd hoped would happen was happening. Their tight little group was unraveling.

"You were extremely jealous of Kimberly Steffer's

relationship with Ellie, weren't you, Mrs. Steffer?"
I asked Joan.

"I wouldn't say that."

"But Kimberly was aware of it. There are many
entries in her diary that refer to it. You hated Mark's
new wife. Resented her creative success."

"You bet I hated her."

"And that's why she killed Mark," Nancy Antonio
said. "I want a lawyer."

"Sure," Josephs said. "As soon as I take you and
your friends downtown and charge you with the
murder of Mark Steffer."

As Josephs started the process of herding the
three of them from the restaurant, I stopped Nancy
Antonio by placing my hand on her arm. "What I
can't figure out, Ms. Antonio, is why *you* wanted
Mark dead."

She looked deep into my eyes. All the forceful
posturing I'd experienced in the hotel lobby was
gone. Two elongated teardrops left tracks on her
face as they left her eyes and ran to her chin. "It
was him," she said, looking at Robert Frederickson.
"I was in love with Robert, and would have done
anything for him. He got me into this mess. He
figured that if Mark was dead, and we could successfully frame Kimberly for the murder, Robert
would get the business for himself, which he did.
He promised me we'd be married once Mark was
out of the way. He lied. The only thing I got was
cancer."

Once outside, Detective Josephs displayed a rare

smile and slapped George on the back. "Nice job, George. Real nice."

George ignored the compliment.

"Hey, Mrs. Fletcher. What about my manuscript?"

"I'll return it to you in the morning," I said. "In the meantime, I suggest you not give up your day job." His grin was now wide and warm. "Yeah. Not very good, huh? Well, writing about murder is your game. Me? I'm better at the real thing."

My raised eyebrows caused him to add, "You're not bad, either—at the real thing. Have a nice night you two. Yeah, I figure you will. Good night."

Chapter Twenty-three

We were picked up at Bangor Airport by Jake Monroe, owner of Cabot Cove's largest taxi service. That the service involved only Jake and his brother, Billy, and two cars, indicated the size of Jake's competitors.

George Sutherland looked out the window as Jake entered town and headed for my house. It was a pristine Maine day, sunny and cool. The heat wave that had gripped the state when I left for San Francisco was probably making someone else's life miserable.

Jake pulled into my driveway.

"No place like home," I said with a contented sigh.

"I can see why you feel that way," George said. "Cabot Cove is a charming village. What a pretty house."

"Thank you," I said after signing Jake Monroe's voucher for the trip. Because I don't drive, I'm Jake's best customer, and have an account with him.

"Brrrr," I said as George put down our bags in

282 Jessica Fletcher and Donald Bain

the foyer. "Let me turn up the heat. So damp. It may be summer, but the house gets damp when I'm gone."

"Like Scotland," George said.

"So I've heard."

"Hopefully, you'll learn firsthand."

I took his tweed topcoat and hung it in the closet. "Make yourself at home, George. Everything's ready for a fire. Just needs a match put to it."

He ignited the newspapers and wood in the fire-place, and sat on a couch in the living room. "What can I get you?" I called from the kitchen. "Scotch? Glass of wine?"

"Scotch would be splendid, thanks."

I was in the process of getting our drinks when George announced from the other room, "There's someone at the door."

"Get it please. My hands are wet."

"Surprise!" I heard two male voices say. No doubt who the voices belonged to. I ran into the living room to greet Sheriff Mort Metzger and Dr. Seth Hazlitt, my two best friends in Cabot Cove, who stood on the front porch, quizzical expressions on their faces.

"Oh," I said. "Sorry. Mort, Seth, I'd like you to meet my good friend, George Sutherland." George extended his hand to Mort, who shook it. Seth had a problem because of the fruit basket. I took it from him, and he and George engaged in a firm handshake.

"Let's not stand here like this," I said. "Come in. I missed you. We just arrived. Jake picked us up in

Bangor. I was just about to call you. I was dying for you to meet George. I—" I realized I'd been talking nonstop from front door to living room. "Thanks for the fruit," I said. "Back in a minute." I went to the kitchen with the basket, leaving my three male friends standing in front of the roaring fire.

"I understand you're an officer with Scotland Yard," Seth said.

"That's the truth," George replied. "Stationed in London. Scottish by birth."

"Had a good friend used to live here who was Scotch," Mort said. I heard it from the kitchen and wondered if George would correct him as he had Detective Josephs. I needn't have worried. It wasn't George's style to create an uncomfortable situation with my friends.

I made drinks for all and rejoined them. "George will be staying here for a few days before he heads home," I said.

"Heah?" Seth said. "In your house?"

"Yes. I want to show off Cabot Cove to him. You'll have a chance to really get to know each other."

"I look forward to that," Mort said, laughing. "Anytime you want, come down and spend some time at the station. Show you how we police here in Maine."

"I appreciate that, Sheriff," George said. "I'll take you up on it."

I wasn't sure how long they planned to stay. But an hour later the four of us were seated at my dining room table enjoying clam chowder and a clam pie from Sassi's Bakery that I'd bought before leaving on my trip.

"Glad to see this travelin' Gypsy lady hasn't forgotten her roots," Seth said as he helped himself to another slice of pie.

"No fear of that," I said.

"What's that stuff you Scotch people like to eat?" Mort asked.

George shot me a glance and a smile before replying, "You're probably referring to *haggis*."

"Ayuh," Mort said. "That's it. Understand it's not for everybody's taste."

"Including mine," George said. "I never learned to enjoy a dish made of minced heart, lungs, and liver of a sheep. They add suet, onions, oatmeal, and some seasonings, then boil it up in the dead sheep's stomach."

There was silence at the table.

"Sorry," George said.

"More pie?" I asked.

"Had my fill," Seth said.

"Not hungry anymore," Mort said.

"So tell me again, Jess, about almost gettin' pushed off the Golden Gate."

"I'll leave that for George," I said, standing and picking up dirty dishes.

"Give you a hand?" they said in unison.

"No. You gentlemen stay put. Tell them all about it, George."

I listened from the kitchen as George filled in

Mort and Seth about my—our—San Francisco adventure.

". . . Jessica became so involved in trying to clear Kimberly Steffer, she dismissed her own near-death experience," George told them. "We learned just before leaving San Francisco that the *bleck* was a local hoodlum hired by Mark Steffer's former partner, Robert Frederickson."

"A bleck?" Mort said.

"A nasty fellow. A term we—Scotch—often use."

"Uh-huh," Seth said. "A some-ugly fella."

"If you say so, Doctor Hazlitt. By the way, Jessica told you about Ms. Steffer's former illustrator falling to his death from the bridge the same morning as her unfortunate incident."

"Ayuh, she did," Seth said.

"The police out there have decided that he jumped, just as his former male lover described it."

"That threesome finally confess?" Mort asked.

"Indirectly. They keep pointing their fingers at each other. Adds up to a confession. I don't think a jury will have trouble convicting them."

"That's good to hear," Mort said. "I suppose Miss Kimberly Steffer is one happy lady these days."

"That's for certain. We had dinner with her and her stepdaughter, Ellie, just last night. They're both happy, and grateful I might add, for Jessica's interest and determination to clear Kimberly. As you can imagine, Jessica Fletcher is a very popular lady with Kimberly and Ellie Steffer."

Eventually, jet lag overtook me, and my yawns

became more frequent. Seth and Mort picked up on my fatigue and prepared to leave. I accompanied George upstairs where he placed his suitcase in one of two spare bedrooms. I preceded him downstairs.

"So, where are you off to next, Jess?" Seth asked.

"Scotland," George answered as he came down the stairs. "Jessica will be spending the Christmas holidays with me at my home in Wick, Scotland. Give her a chance to see my hometown and meet some of my family and friends. We'll probably sneak some time in London for a show or two."

Mort and Seth said good night, but not before George arranged to visit Mort's police headquarters in the morning. When they were gone, George suggested a nightcap. Brandy snifters in hand, we clinked rims: "To a successful resolution of the Kimberly Steffer case," he said.

"Definitely worth raising our glasses to," I said.

"I have the feeling I shouldn't have announced your plans to visit Scotland over the holidays."

"Oh, they'll get over it. They like us all to be together at Christmas."

"I can understand that."

"I think they're more upset that you're staying in my house while you're here in Cabot Cove."

"Yes. I sensed that. Perhaps it would be better if I stayed in a hotel. I'm sure you have some very nice ones."

"Oh, yes, we certainly do. And I don't want to hear another word about that. This is where you shall stay, Inspector Sutherland. I've never had a—a Scotchman as a houseguest before."

We both laughed.

"Go to bed and have a fair night's sleep, Jessica," he said. "To paraphrase Robbie Burns, *'My Jessica's asleep by thy murmuring stream; Flow gently sweet Afton, disturb not her dream.'* "

For a dish of
baked beans and murder
don't miss the next
Murder, She Wrote mystery:

A DEADLY JUDGMENT
by Jessica Fletcher and Donald Bain

Cafe Pamplona's outdoor terrace had become crowded since I'd taken a table and ordered a shrimp cocktail and glass of sparkling water. I'd spent the late afternoon in Cambridge's Harvard Square, enjoying its vibrant mix of students, professorial types, foreigners, panhandlers, and protestors. Now, it was time to make a tough decision. Should I attempt to contact Professor Montrose to warn him of the potential danger he might be facing? If so, I would again be disobeying the court's order forbidding members of either the defense or prosecution from making contact with jurors in the Billy Brannigan murder trial.

But if I didn't—and my suspicions were correct—Professor Montrose, Juror Number Four, might end up dead like the other two, the most recent "accident" being Juror Number Seven.

Making contact with the family of Juror Number Seven had been, I knew, not only a serious breach of legal ethics, it undoubtedly broke the law. Many laws. Had my foray into South Boston become known to the stern Judge Wilson, pleading ignorance of the law wouldn't get me very far, probably no further than a jail cell. Charge? Contempt of court. "Lock her up and throw away the key."

As part of Malcolm McLoon's team defending accused murderer Billy Brannigan, I'd become "an officer of the court" in a sense. Once I'd agreed to become one of Malcolm's jury consultants, a decision I'd been debating ever since arriving in Boston, I was expected to play by the rules set down by the judge. Her words reverberated in my head:

"Under no circumstance is anyone involved in the case, from either the defense or prosecution, to have any contact, of any nature, written, oral or through third parties, with any member of the twelve-person jury, or the six alternates. Because I have faith in each juror's integrity and honesty, and because the attorneys representing the people and the defendant are known to me to uphold the highest professional standards"—the judge winced when including McLoon in that group—"I have decided against sequestering this jury. Its members are admonished to not read about the case or hear reports about it through radio or television, and are not to discuss the case with anyone until it has been submitted to them. And I reiterate—no person from either side is to have any personal contact with members of the jury."

But, I rationalized, Juror Number Seven was alive when Judge Wilson issued that order.

Excerpt from A DEADLY JUDGMENT

Juror Number Seven had been an attractive, thirty-four-year-old woman with two children, a sickly mother-in-law for whom she cared, and a husband who worked as a construction foreman. She enjoyed painting by the numbers, baking, and collecting seashells. I liked her the moment she started answering questions during *voir dire*, that pretrial ritual where the attorneys from each side question prospective jurors to ferret out hidden prejudices, veiled biases, or life circumstances creating a conflict of interest. She was straightforward in her answers, someone who would take her duties as a juror seriously, especially where the accused faced the rest of his life in prison. I didn't hesitate telling Malcolm that, in my judgment, she was the sort of fair-minded person we wanted on the jury. That hadn't set well with the expensive *professional* jury consultant Malcolm had hired, who resented my inclusion from the moment Malcolm introduced me. "Jessica is an astute judge of character," he'd said in his usual bombastic style. "While I appreciate your expertise in these matters, Jessica's gut feelings as a bestselling author and observer of life matter a great deal to me—and, I might add, to the accused." His speech was met with grim smiles by the woman being paid more than one hundred thousand dollars to study community attitudes and demographic patterns, her "scientific" findings contained in boxes filled with computer printouts.

She hadn't liked Juror Number Seven. But my instinctive positive evaluation of her held more water with Malcolm, and she was accepted on the jury.

And now she was dead, run down by a hit-and-run driver in front of her modest home as she returned from buying milk and bread at a local convenience store. The second death on the jury in a week. Something was wrong, and I was determined to find out what it was.

I arrived at Juror Number Seven's house as her husband and mother-in-law were about to leave for the wake. Her husband was a broad, beefy man with a workman's hands and large, sad brown eyes. His mother sat stoically in a wheelchair, rosary beads clutched tightly in her gnarled fingers.

"I'm sorry to intrude like this," I said. "My name is Jessica Fletcher."

The husband cocked his head and narrowed his eyes. "The mystery writer?"

"Yes. I'm also a consultant to Billy Brannigan's defense team."

"I know that," he said. "We read about you. My wife said—" He turned away as his eyes moistened.

"I'm so sorry about what happened," I said. "I didn't know your wife, but I liked her the minute she started answering questions from the lawyers. I knew she'd make a fine juror."

He wiped his cheek with the back of his hand. "Maybe if she hadn't been on that damn jury she'd still be alive," he said.

"Do you think her death had something to do with being a juror?" I asked. My rising inflection wasn't genuine. I, too, had the feeling her jury duty was linked in some way to being run down.

"All I know is she was alive before the trial started. Now, she's laid out, about to be put in the ground."

"That's why I've come here," I said. "I know she was killed by a hit-and-run driver. Is there anything to lead you to believe it might have been deliberate?"

"Seems to me it was," he replied. "She was up on the curb when it happened. Seems to me he had to aim for her to hit her there."

"Yes," I said, "it does seem that way. Did you have any indication as to how she was leaning as a juror?"

His face became angry. "Is that why you're here, trying to find out whether she thought that Brannigan brat is guilty of murdering his own brother?"

"Only to see if what I'm thinking about your wife's death, and the death of the other juror might be true. The other juror who died seemed to believe in Billy Brannigan's innocence. But I take it from what you've just said that your wife didn't."

"Jurors aren't supposed to talk about the case with anybody, including family."

"I know, but it's human nature to—"

"She talked about it."

"And?"

"She didn't think he did it. Killed his brother. I tried to talk sense to her but . . . I don't suppose I should be telling you this, but it doesn't seem to make any difference anymore. The judge can't do anything to hurt her."

"So your wife was leaning in favor of the defendant. Like the other juror."

"Brannigan'll get off. People with money always do."

Juror Number Seven's mother-in-law had sat silently during my conversation with her son. Now, she looked up at me and said, "She was a good woman. Like my own daughter. May God shine his light on her."

I swallowed the lump in my throat, thanked them for allowing me to intrude in their time of grief, and quickly walked away.

There were two dead jurors, each having indicated to a family member they'd been inclined to acquit Billy Brannigan. If my read on Professor Montrose, Juror Number Four, was correct—that he, too, was buying Malcolm McLoon's defense of Brannigan—another unfortunate "accident" could be in the offing.

I paid my check at Cafe Pamplona, confirmed Montrose's address from a slip of paper in my purse, and slowly walked in the direction of his street, which was only a few blocks away. Darkness was falling; lights came to life in shops and the area's many university buildings. I paused at the corner.

Last chance to change your mind, Jess. You've been lucky so far that no one's reported you to the court. Let it go. You're probably wrong anyway. Just a coin-

cidence that two members of the same jury panel have died. Just a coincidence that both appeared to favor the defendant. You're in Boston as a jury consultant, not to prove a conspiracy. You came here because an old friend, attorney Malcolm McLoon, asked you to come, and because you wanted to soak up the atmosphere of a real murder trial to use in your next murder mystery. Give it up, Jess. Go back to your lovely hotel suite, take a Jacuzzi, read a good book and—

I stood opposite Professor Montrose's six-story apartment building, drew a deep breath, and looked up the one-way street. A car slowly approached; plenty of time for me to cross. But as I stepped off the curb, the sudden roar of its engine froze me in my tracks. I turned. The car was bearing down on me at racetrack speed. I twisted and hurled myself back in the direction of the curb, landing with a thud on the pavement, my cheek making painful contact with the concrete. The car, large and dark in color—brown? black? blue?—flashed by in a blur, its left tire missing my foot by less than an inch.

I didn't give Professor Montrose, Juror Number Four, another thought until the smiling young doctor in Harvard University Hospital's emergency room assured me my face was only scraped and bruised, nothing broken. By then, I wanted only to get back to my suite at the Omni Parker House, lock the door and shut the drapes against the outside world and all its potential violence. Before I could, however, the police wanted to question me about the incident. I told them everything I could remember, which wasn't much. One thing I was sure of, I said. The driver of that dark car had deliberately tried to run me down.

"What were you doing on that particular street, Mrs. Fletcher?" one officer asked.

"I was—just sightseeing."

"That's a residential street," he said. "Nothing touristy."

"A pretty street," I said. "I just sort of wandered down it."

"You're on the Brannigan defense team," his partner said as they prepared to drive me back to the hotel.

"That's right."

"My wife's been watching the trial on *Court TV*."

"Oh? I'm not sure I agree with allowing television cameras into the courtroom," I said, gingerly touching my fingertips to my stinging cheekbone. "But then again, there is the public's right to know what goes on in its justice system."

"Shame how those jurors died," he said, holding open the rear door of the marked police car.

"Terrible," I agreed.

He and his partner got in the front seat. The engine came to life and we pulled into Boston traffic. "Yeah," the officer said, turning his head to speak directly to me. "Really strange, three people from the same jury dying like that."

It took a moment for his words to sink in. When

they did, I sprang forward and placed my hands on his shoulders. "Did you say *three*?"

"Yes, ma'am. That's why I was interested in how come you were on that street when you were. That professor on the jury—Number Four I think was his number—fell off his roof just a little after you almost got run down."

"Fell—off—his—roof?"

"Yup. Or got pushed."

I slumped back in the seat and pressed my fingers to my temples. The stinging on my cheek had been replaced by a pounding, pulsating pain deep inside my head. I'd been right. It was no longer just a theory. Three members of the Billy Brannigan jury had died in less than a week. I believe in coincidence. I think it happens more than we realize.

But there's coincidence, and then there's coincidence.

Somebody was killing off the jurors, and it looked like only those who were sympathetic to the defense were marked for an accident.

And then it dawned on me that it wasn't only jurors who were in jeopardy. This jury consultant had almost become coincidence number four.

"Could you drive a little faster?" I said. "I have some very important phone calls to make."